PENGUIN BOOKS

THE BEGGAR'S PAWN

John L'Heureux was a novelist, short story writer, and poet who taught at Stanford University for several decades, heading the Wallace Stegner Creative Writing Fellowship for many of them. His stories have appeared in the *New Yorker* and other publications, and his novels include *A Woman Run Mad*, *The Shrine at Altamira*, and *The Medici Boy*. He was a Jesuit before publishing his first novel, *Tight White Collar*, in 1972. He died in 2019.

Photo by Dagmar Logie

THE
BEGGAR'S PAWN

❖ ❖ ❖

JOHN L'HEUREUX

PENGUIN BOOKS

PENGUIN BOOKS

An imprint of Penguin Random House LLC

penguinrandomhouse.com

Library of Congress Cataloging-in-Publication Data

Names: L'Heureux, John, author.
Title: The beggar's pawn / John L'Heureux.
Description: New York : Penguin Books, 2020. |
Identifiers: LCCN 2020004063 (print) | LCCN 2020004064 (ebook) |
ISBN 9780143135234 (trade paperback) | ISBN 9780525506911 (ebook)
Classification: LCC PS3562.H4 B44 2020 (print) | LCC PS3562.H4 (ebook) |
DDC 813/.54--dc23
LC record available at https://lccn.loc.gov/2020004063
LC ebook record available at https://lccn.loc.gov/2020004064

Printed in the United States of America
1 3 5 7 9 10 8 6 4 2

BOOK DESIGN BY LUCIA BERNARD

For our friend Deborah Treisman

Contents

❖ ❖ ❖

THE
BEGGAR'S PAWN

PART ONE

❖　❖　❖

1.

They first met Reginald Parker ages ago—in the innocent part of the year 2001—before disaster struck at the World Trade Center and the Pentagon and an empty field in Shanksville, Pennsylvania, at a time when it was still possible to think ours was a virtuous country and everyone liked us and terrorists were just a plot complication in the movies. We had no idea then what forms terrorism could take, at home and away, in that innocent time ages ago.

Anyhow, they met Reginald Parker while they were out walking their new puppy, Dickens. They were David and Maggie Holliss, and Dickens was not actually their puppy but their son Sedge's. They were dog-sitting for Dickens while Sedge went through the ritual of getting a divorce. It was his fourth divorce and the Hollisses were not happy about it, but they liked the puppy and they were pleased when Reginald Parker stopped them and said, "What a wonderful little dog. What do you call him?"

"He's still a puppy," Maggie said, "but he's house-trained." This was partly true.

"We call him Dickens," David said.

"Dickens as in Charles? Or as in, 'He's a little dickens'?"

"Charles, I think," Maggie said. "He's got a bookish look to him, that little face. He's part Labrador retriever."

"Well, he's a wonderful little dog. Puppy." He scratched the dog's ears and then the soft fur on his chest. "Good Dickens. Nice Dickens." He smiled at them as David tugged lightly at the leash. "So long, Dickens."

They were on their way to the local dog park and when they were safely out of earshot Maggie said, "He seems very nice."

"His hair is too long," David said. "And he's intrusive."

"He's good looking, in a way," Maggie said.

"He needs a shave."

Maggie gave him one of her looks. "I thought he seemed very nice," she said.

That was how they first met Reginald Parker.

THEY MET HIM FOR the second time a few days later, again while they were taking Dickens to the dog park.

"My old friend Dickens," he said, and knelt down beside the dog to fondle his ears. Dickens gave a tentative lick to his face. Reginald had not shaved since they last met.

"I didn't realize why he was called Dickens," Reginald said. "I didn't realize you were Professor Holliss. I should have, though. Practically everybody around here is a professor of something or other. But I didn't put two and two together, your specialty and the dog's name."

"Are you growing a beard?" David asked.

"It's very becoming," Maggie said. "Or it will be."

Reginald stood up and fingered his bristly chin. "I'm a writer," he said. "I figured it goes with the territory."

"A writer!" Maggie said. "Yes. Yes. What do you write?"

"I'm working on a novel right now."

"A novel!" Maggie looked at David, who said nothing. "How exciting!"

"Well, I haven't published yet," Reginald said. "You know what the publishing industry is like these days. Nobody wants novels. All they want is memoirs of my life as a drug addict."

"Oh, dear," Maggie said.

"Not *my* life. I've never been a drug addict. Not really, I mean. I mean that's the kind of thing they want. You must find that, too, in your field, Professor Holliss. No?"

"No. Nobody wants to know about my drug addiction."

They all laughed, nervous, and Dickens barked as if he understood.

"I'm Reg Parker," Reginald said, sticking out his hand, "and you're Professor Holliss, I know, and you must be Mrs. Holliss."

They shook hands and said hello, yes, hello.

"I'm a great admirer of your work on Dickens," Reginald said.

"Thackeray, you mean," David said. "My only work on Dickens is trying to get him not to pee on the kitchen floor."

David Holliss was known for his work on Thackeray and had been briefly famous for his work on Stephen Crane. But now, late in his career, it was Thackeray whom people seemed to remember though they often confused him with Dickens.

"Thackeray, of course, I meant Thackeray. Sorry about that."

"People do that all the time. Maybe it means I should work on Dickens."

"He's working on Gissing now," Maggie said.

"Gissing?"

"*New Grub Street* Gissing. The writer as a kind of production-line worker. Poverty. Desperation." She paused. "The long climb from lower-middle to upper-middle class. It's great stuff."

"Maybe we could talk about your writing sometime," Reginald said. "I'd like that."

David took a step backward. "Thanks for the offer, but I never talk about writing while it's in progress. Foolish of me, probably, but I just don't. Besides, I'm still doing research. But thanks. And good luck with the novel. I admire anybody who undertakes a novel. It's like signing up for . . . well, I don't know what . . . a suicide mission, I guess. We've gotta get moving."

As if on command Dickens bolted after a squirrel and was tugged back by his leash. "See," David said.

And so they left Reginald Parker and continued their walk.

"A suicide mission?" Maggie said.

"Nosey Parker," David said.

They walked in silence for a while, pausing to let Dickens savor all the delicious smells left by other dogs.

"Good boy," David said as Dickens lifted his leg on a holly bush.

"You weren't very friendly," Maggie said.

"He's lonely, is all."

"Poor soul," Maggie said.

David said nothing until they got home. Then he said what he had kept himself from saying during the whole long walk. "You shouldn't have told him about Gissing. My work is private. You know that."

"I'm sorry."

"I'm still researching. I still haven't read all his novels. Who knows, I may never write the damned book."

"I've said I'm sorry."

"It's too late to be sorry."

"If you can hold on a minute, I'll go and kill myself."

"Do you see what he's caused, that Parker? We're fighting and we never fight. That man is trouble."

BUT PARKER WASN'T TROUBLE, at least not then, in the innocent part of the year 2001. After that one conversation he seemed to understand that David's writing was off-limits and so he let it alone. The dog, however, was not only a safe topic, it was a welcome one. Over the next months the three of them met often on their morning walks. Dickens would bound forward, tugging at the leash, eager for the pats and chest rubs of his new bearded friend.

"I just love this dog," Reginald said.

"I'm surprised you don't get one of your own," Maggie said. "They make a morning walk a lot more enjoyable." She had come to the conclusion that he was a bachelor, starving for his art, and he needed a dog as a companion. On the other hand perhaps his morning walks were in service of his novel, a kind of thinking time before he sat down to write, and so a dog might prove to be a distraction. She'd have liked to ask him about this, but she worried that any talk of writing would lead to questions about David's work on Gissing and thus to unhappiness at home.

"I could never afford a dog," Reginald said. "Not a beauty like Dickens. Could I, Dickens? No, I couldn't. Never." And he gave the dog a firm pat on the behind.

Later, Maggie said to David, "He could never afford a dog. That's what he said."

David recognized the tone and could tell she was thinking of buying him one.

"Don't," he said. "Let sleeping dogs et cetera."

ONE DAY WHEN DAVID was not feeling up to a walk—he had thrown his back out while putting on his shoes—Maggie took Dickens to the park by herself and, as she thought she might, she ran into Reginald Parker. He was walking with his head down, apparently lost in thought, and it was only when Dickens poked his cold nose into Reginald's hand that he looked up, surprised, and greeted them both.

"Thinking of your book?" Maggie asked.

"Book?" he said. He looked confused.

"The novel," she said. And then, "I always forget. Writers don't like to talk about their work in progress." She noticed that his pupils were dilated as if he were on something, and she remembered Sedge when he was high on grass.

"I was a friend of Iris Murdoch," Reginald said.

"Really! How exciting. Did she talk about her work in progress?"

"To her friends, she did."

"Well, that is exciting. Iris Murdoch. *A Severed Head. The Black Prince.* I love Murdoch."

"I have to go," he said.

Maggie couldn't wait to get home and tell David that Reginald Parker, however strange he might be, was in fact a friend of Iris Murdoch.

"How's that possible? She's dead."

"Well, he was, I mean."

"Maybe there's more to him than we think," David said. "Iris Murdoch. Really?"

Maggie did not mention that Reginald had been high on grass. Or something.

OVER THE NEXT YEARS David continued to pick away at his research on Gissing and, so they imagined, Reginald Parker continued to write his novel. They talked about him from time to time when they ran into him on their morning walks, but other than that they gave him no thought whatsoever. When they did meet, always by chance, Dickens remained their common interest and, except for the weather, their only topic of conversation.

One morning Reginald walked back with them to their home.

"What a huge house," he said. "I had no idea."

"We've been here forever," Maggie said, embarrassed, since there was too much house for just the two of them. "All the kids grew up here."

"It's beautiful without looking pretentious," Reginald said. "Not like some of them."

They didn't know what to say and so they said nothing.

"I live in the guest cottage behind the Lorings. You know their house?"

"We know the Lorings, to say hello," David said. "Very nice people."

"He's at the law school," Maggie said. "It's a very big house."

"For just the two of them," Reginald said. "And he says he's a Marxist. So much for theory and practice." He seemed to want to say more but he just looked at them.

"Well, it's been lovely," Maggie said.

David gave him the offhand wave that signaled goodbye.

He watched them go up the driveway to the back entrance of the house and then—thinking what?—he turned away.

THE HOLLISSES AND PARKER remained acquaintances merely. They were not friends. They did not drop in for neighborly visits. They were academic types living in Professorville—a neighborhood of academics—and the neighbors felt no need to socialize. And everyone, everyone who mattered, preferred it this way. Then, in 2009, there came a moment when their relationship changed.

Maggie had gone to the front door to get a parcel from the

UPS man and stood examining the label when suddenly Dickens wiggled past her and dashed down the front walk after a squirrel. The squirrel made for the live oak in front of the house, and from a high branch it dropped to the ground and streaked across the pavement to a tree on the opposite side of the street. Dickens pursued the squirrel frantically and stood beneath the tree barking in frustration and wagging his tail. Maggie looked up and down the street, saw there were no cars coming, and called the dog home. "Good boy," she shouted, "come on, Dickens! Come on!" Eventually Dickens gave up on the treed squirrel and started across the street toward her. At that moment the UPS driver put his truck in gear and began to move slowly forward. Dickens was crossing toward Maggie but paused to look back toward the squirrel. And at that moment the UPS truck sped up. Maggie screamed, "No!" and Dickens turned back to her. Out of nowhere—she had seen no cars, nobody walking— Reginald Parker suddenly appeared in the street in front of the truck and threw himself bodily between the truck and the dog, shouting, "Stop! Stop!" The brakes squealed and the truck came to a dead halt but not before Reginald was flung against its window and then back onto the pavement. The dog sprang free. The UPS man slumped over his wheel and Maggie stood frozen at the front door while Dickens, his belly flat to the grass, approached her on his front paws. Reginald lay in the road, motionless.

The driver did not move and Maggie did not move until finally, slowly, Reginald's arms twitched, and then his legs, and then he sat up. Everyone came back to life.

The UPS man got out of his truck and ran over to Reginald, saying, "Don't move. Just lie flat," even though he could see Reginald was already sitting up. Maggie let the door slam behind her and dashed down the path to the street. And Dickens, no longer to blame, ran to Reginald and pressed his wet muzzle against his neck.

"I'm fine," Reginald said. "I'm just shaken." But the palms of both hands were scraped and bleeding.

Dickens nosed about after Maggie, uncertain what was expected of him. She patted him and rubbed him all over to make sure he was okay and then she turned her attention to Reginald.

She and the UPS man helped him to his feet. Reginald stood for a minute, getting his balance, and then, each with an arm around him, they walked him up the path into the house. They settled him, cautiously, on the living room couch. Maggie got a bowl of hot water and a tube of Neosporin and a roll of cotton gauze, and when she returned, the UPS man, frantic still, made it clear that he was eager to go. He left. Reginald sat quietly, his hands on his knees with his palms turned up, looking around him and taking in the grand piano, the comfy furniture, the paintings of family: the Hollisses with their three children when they were still babies, and then, separately, each of the children painted when they were in their teens. A huge bay window looked out over the back garden.

"I'm so sorry," Maggie said, kneeling at his side and sponging his scraped palms with a clean white towel. "It's my fault," she said. "I should have been watching him more closely."

Reginald said nothing. He sat back and let her wash his palms and smear them with Neosporin and wrap them in gauze.

She finished and sat back on her heels. "There," she said, and Reginald sighed and shut his eyes, content, as if he might stay like this for the rest of the day.

She remained kneeling before him, startled into silence by her growing realization that he was on some kind of drug. But it was probably just grass. It was probably just a painkiller. She stood up and waited for him to say something. He sat there with his eyes closed.

"If you're all right," she said, "I could drive you home."

He said nothing but only opened his eyes.

"You shouldn't be walking after that upset."

He smiled as Dickens placed a paw upon his knee.

"You're sure you're all right? Do you think I should take you to the emergency room?"

"It's so peaceful here," Reginald said.

She sat beside him on the couch. Dickens curled up at their feet.

Maggie stood up finally and took the bowl of water out to the kitchen. He was all right, he had only been shaken up, but now he seemed to want to stay here and rest. She was strangely uncomfortable with this, and yet surely she owed him more than a couple of bandages. He had saved her dog's life.

"We'll have a coffee," she said, "and then I'll drive you home."

They had coffee and Reginald got himself together and stood for a moment looking beyond the grand piano out into the back garden. "I didn't know you had a pool," he said.

"It's only a little thing," she said. "Mostly decorative, but David likes to do mini-laps after he's done his work for the day."

"It must be nice," Reginald said. He continued to stand looking out. "You have everything."

Maggie felt guilty suddenly—she felt accused—and then, just as suddenly, she felt a rush of gratitude for his throwing himself at the UPS truck and saving Dickens. They did indeed have everything and he very likely had nothing.

"If there is ever anything we can do to thank you," she said, "please . . ." And, almost before she could finish the sentence, he said, "Well, there *is* something." He cleared his throat and apologized and then started to speak again and almost at once he said, "No, I can't ask, really, I shouldn't." But finally he got it out.

"Could you loan me two hundred dollars?"

It was an emergency, he explained, it was one of those things that just happens, and he could tell her the whole story if she wanted him to, but it was embarrassing, it was humiliating to have to ask for money. It was a loan only, he would pay her back within a week, maybe sooner, but he *would* repay it, he promised.

"Absolutely," Maggie said. "Absolutely," and she got her checkbook.

Reginald was still asking and promising and apologizing by the time Maggie finished writing the check. He folded it in half and slipped it into his breast pocket.

He was eager to go now and Maggie drove him home.

She decided she would not mention the loan to David, though that same evening she told him at length and with a vivid sense of drama how Reginald had thrown himself in front of the UPS truck and saved Dickens's life. She cried as she talked about it and David was near tears himself.

"Reginald Parker," he said. "Who would believe it?" And the more he thought about it, the more he felt moved to thank Reginald formally, appropriately. The next day he went to Whole Foods and put together a basket of champagne and red caviar and paté, several excellent cheeses, and an assortment of tinned meats. It was a picnic hamper for an extravagant afternoon at the beach, it was slightly crazy, and he had it delivered to Reginald with a note of thanks. It cost nearly three hundred dollars— but only think if they'd lost Dickens!—and David decided he would not mention it to Maggie.

It was 2009 and the stock market was in the pits and the less you said about money the better.

2.

As it happened, Reginald Parker returned the two hundred dollars in just over a week. He returned it in cash—ten twenties—which Maggie found embarrassing, but Reginald didn't seem to notice her embarrassment; in fact, he seemed to want to linger over the transaction.

"I'm an honest creditor," he said, "I pay my bills," and he counted out his ten twenty-dollar bills.

David was in his study reading Gissing's *The Odd Women* and Maggie was grateful he was not witness to this.

MAGGIE AND DAVID HOLLISS were sixty-five years old when they first met Reginald Parker in the year 2001 and for some time David had been talking about retirement. "Nobody wants an old teacher," he would say. "Everybody talks about wisdom and experience and all that crap, but when it comes down to it, young people want to be taught by their own kind. They want somebody they can look up to, but only a little, somebody ten years older and ten times better looking."

"But you love teaching," Maggie would say.

"You've got to know when to quit," he said again. And again.

He still hadn't quit some five years later when he turned seventy. It was easy just to go along teaching his two courses in fall and two in winter and to spend spring and summer researching and traveling and lazing about. The students seemed interested still, and he had a couple of PhD dissertations to direct, which made him feel legal, he said, and the money was good, so why not just continue on. He could go on researching the Gissing book forever—it would see him to his grave perhaps—and so what the hell.

Then, when he turned seventy-one, the tax laws obliged him to start withdrawing money from his retirement plan. "I'm old," he said to Maggie, "and we've got plenty of money. I should do the decent thing and retire."

She wasn't sure how life would be with him hanging around the house, but she said, "Whatever you want," and when he gave her that doubtful look of his, she said, "Just don't start invading the kitchen." And a little later she said, "You've earned the right to do whatever you want."

It was out of old habit that she liked to emphasize his earnings because at the start of their marriage she had been rich and he had felt guilty about it. Her money had bought their house and her money had made it possible for him to take an academic job that paid only half their yearly expenses. Maggie was a Sedgwick, admittedly from the poor branch, and when her parents died they left practically nothing. A doting great-aunt, however, had left Maggie a trust fund of a little under two million from which she was paid ten thousand a year until she was twenty-five, at which time the entire capital became hers: small by Sedgwick standards but a vast fortune in an academic community. David felt guilty buying the house with Maggie's money—fifty thousand was a huge sum back then—but he found the guilt easier to live with as each year went by.

They were healthy and happy in Northern California. The weather, always benign, seemed to encourage people to be active, and so with tennis and swimming and long daily walks they seemed immune—even at age seventy-one—to the absurdities of old age. No shaking hand, no halting speech, no blank stare at being suddenly lost. They suffered only the usual health surprises of young old age. Maggie had had a hysterectomy at forty and a cancer scare at sixty. David, with no physical problems to speak of, had a small stroke at sixty, an attention getter, and a milder one at sixty-three, a reminder. Consequently both of them were keen on staying fit and young, or youngish. Maggie retained her thin figure by eating only half of every meal, a practice she had observed since she was a teen. David, on the other hand, had begun to put on weight around his middle, though at six feet three he was able to carry the extra pounds. He had a mass of gray hair and broad shoulders and his eyes were wide, making him seem pleasantly surprised. In short, they looked like what they were: a couple suspended between middle and old age, happy, wealthy, content. And comfortably godless.

"Religion makes him nervous," Maggie said. Like all the Sedgwicks, she had been baptized in the Church of England, but the baptism hadn't taken and she was perfectly happy with David's gentlemanly atheism.

"There's been more blood spilled in the name of religion . . ." David began and the sentence might end anywhere, ". . . than over money . . . than over land . . . than over power . . ." whatever came to mind at that moment. He had a positive fear of religion. "All religions are dangerous," he said. Churches and church services put him off completely. He had been an atheist because he had been raised that way, shielded from superstition by a devoted mother and an uninterested father and insulated against theology of any sort by a nicely secular education, first at Harvard, then at Yale. He had an acute moral sense nevertheless; he was politically liberal and he had a rigorous understanding of right and wrong. Long ago, in his first year of teaching, he had lost patience with a particularly difficult student in freshman comp—exasperated at her resistance to basic grammar, he told her she was not only uneducated, she was uneducable as well—and he remained apologetic about it for the next ten years. He paid his taxes to the last penny. He supported all the right causes and made generous contributions to a large number of clamoring charities. He believed in justice, fidelity, and financial rectitude. He considered himself a genial atheist. Nothing militant about him. It was just religion that made him nervous. That's how he was. Dickens, on the other hand, made him calm.

Dickens was like one of her children, Maggie said, except without all the problems. Dickens chased squirrels, and once he got sprayed by a skunk and they'd had to wash him down with tomato juice, but he was an excellent dog, amiable and devoted, and who could help but love him? Their kids had been a different matter. All three of them had been problem children, smart

next three marriages. He had turned out handsome and sexy and—never mind the fluttering hands and the mass of black curls—people were always falling in love with him. He would marry an unsuspecting girl, buy a house—he could always depend on the parents for help in a pinch—and settle down forever with his new bride. Within the next year or two Sedge and his wife would decide it had all been a well-intentioned, glittering mistake, though of course they would remain good friends. Divorce. Division of the spoils. Alimony for a specified time. Never any children so there was no need for child support. Fortunately his job as a research scientist for a Los Angeles pharmaceutical company paid him well, with fat bonuses each year, and his parents could be depended upon to dog-sit while he sorted out his life. This is how they came to have Dickens, and when Sedge saw how they doted on the dog, he didn't have the heart to take him back.

Years passed and Sedge continued to spend too much time on his hair and to wave his hands about when he talked. These habits on more than one occasion gave rise to brief misunderstandings of a sexual nature, usually at cocktail parties where they could be laughed off as a by-product of drink, but Sedge found these situations amusing and, in a way, flattering since he was getting well into middle age and he still hadn't settled down to normal life. What he wanted was his parents' marriage, a meeting of minds and hearts that excluded everybody else, even their children. That last thought surprised him with its coldness and its accuracy. They loved him, just as they loved his younger brother, Will, and his sister, Claire, but not as they loved each other and not as they loved Dickens. For a moment he felt jealous of the dog. And of Will.

Will, in his teens, had become the perfect son. He had started out like the rest of them, adored and indulged and frequently in trouble, and when he was thirteen he had followed Sedge into his high-on-grass period. That didn't last, however, because Will unexpectedly developed a superego that could not reconcile such mindless self-indulgence, as he announced, with the brevity of life and his own seriousness of purpose. There was nothing morally wrong with marijuana; it was just that you lost so much time being out of it and he was convinced that it permanently damaged a person's basic mental acuity.

"Look around you," he said to Sedge. "Look at your friends. They're all losers."

Sedge waved his hands in protest but, failing to find the right put-down, he said, "And you, I suppose, are the Perfect Son."

"Capital, old fruit," Will said, intending to sound British. Will took his new conscience with him to Berkeley, after which he did graduate work in English literature at Essex in England. He married another graduate student—an English girl named Daphne—and, in a particularly hospitable moment, the university offered him a teaching job on the Modern Literature faculty. The couple bought a house with a little help from Maggie and David and immediately produced a child, a daughter, after which they had another daughter every other year until there were three in all. Will wrote his mother and father on the major holidays and phoned them once a month and sent comic greeting cards on their birthdays and their wedding anniversary. He rarely asked them for money, though they sent him whatever they gave the others and they rejoiced that at least one of their children led a loving, well-ordered life. Will's wife collected antique porcelain dolls, each with its own name and wardrobe, but David and Maggie overlooked the dolls since Daphne was a good wife and mother and she was devoted to Will.

It was Claire they worried about.

Their youngest, Claire, was born while Maggie and David were on sabbatical in Italy and, enchanted by everything Italian, they had named her Chiara. But she was never a Chiara, not for a moment. She was Claire, plain, straightforward, definite. As a baby she was a speck of a thing and, though her two brothers were tall and thin, Claire grew up short and chunky. "I'm a block," she said at age ten. "I'm the shortest girl in my class."

"But you're lovely," Maggie said. "You have beautiful eyes."

"And I'm fat," Claire said. "You can't deny it."

What could you do with a child like that?

Early on her teachers protested and then learned to fear her frankness, for which she was praised at home. "You always know what Claire is thinking," the teachers said, "and if you don't, she'll tell you." Indeed her frankness was so often commented on that she came to regard it as a virtue, and cultivated it, and confused it with honesty and integrity. "Claire's fierce integrity" was taken for granted by Maggie and David, who did nothing to tame it.

Thus Claire grew up and went to Columbia and emerged

with her fierce integrity focused on social issues, beginning with race relations and moving on to the inequities of immigration law and the evils of preemptive war. Unable to find a satisfying job, she took up residence in a commune in Oregon and left it after little more than a year because of what she saw as the basic selfishness of the lifestyle. While she was there, however, she found a boyfriend and had a son by him—named Gaius for his father—and almost at once broke off the relationship. She left, but kept in touch. The little boy stayed in the commune with his father. In time—and with the financial help of the Hollisses—Gaius attended Princeton, where he majored in economics.

After her time in the commune, she herself had gone on to a life of near poverty, first with a lesbian partner who had left the commune to become a theater director in Baltimore and then, if Claire had had her way, with the Little Sisters of the Poor in Oklahoma. She made a retreat at their convent and, when the eight days were over, she asked to be admitted as a novice.

The Mother Superior was an old hand at delayed vocations.

"Have you felt this calling for a long time now?"

"I don't have a calling. I don't think I have a calling."

"But you care passionately about good and evil?"

"I have no interest in good and evil. They're abstractions and I'm a practical woman. I'm from California. I care about justice."

"Justice, of course. And charity? You care about charity."

"Where it's deserved."

"Charity is loving-kindness. Charity is a gift of the Spirit of God. It exalts the giver. Like faith, it is a free gift."

"Gifts should be given to those who deserve them."

Mother realized she was on the wrong track.

"Were you raised Catholic or are you a convert?"

In this way Mother Superior discovered that Claire was not a Catholic at all, though she said that if accepted by the order she would be willing to turn Catholic. Mother Superior explained, with a severe show of patience, that Claire would have to turn Catholic first and then, after a probationary period of three years, she could apply to the order and they would—in good time—decide if she was ready for the postulancy.

"Fuck that," Claire claimed to have said, frankly, though at the time she replied that such a probationary period seemed too long. She could be poor on her own, she decided, though she had liked the idea of caring for the old and the ill as the Little Sisters of the Poor did, and she liked their costume. As to caring for the old and the ill, she could take care of Misery and Poop, as she called her mother and father, even though family care lacked the satisfaction that came from caring for strangers. She decided to check in with them—just a short visit—and see how they were doing in their old age, at seventy-something.

They were doing well and pretended to be pleased that Claire had reunited with Willow, the lesbian theater person.

"You're not pleased."

"It's your life, darling. You must do whatever is right for you."

"You like me in my native condition," Claire said. "Alone."

"We like you just as you are," Maggie said. "You have the most beautiful eyes."

David got them drinks and the tension subsided.

"The Little Sisters of the Poor refused me. That's what they're called."

"Aren't they those poor nuns in the Poulenc opera?"

"No, those are Carmelites. Anyhow, you've got to be a Catholic to join. I feel that's just another kind of bigotry. An Old Boys' club, but for Catholic women." She had already begun to turn her experience into an anecdote that might entertain.

Maggie did not know how to reply so she remained silent.

"She was all fired up about charity, the Mother Superior."

More silence.

"I told her that charity has to be earned." Claire thought about this. "She hated me."

"Catholics are strange. They like their own kind."

"Yes, like academics."

They seemed to have run out of conversation already and the visit had hardly begun. Claire was expecting some comment on her weight.

"You've lost some weight," Maggie noticed finally. "You're developing a lovely figure."

"I know, I know . . . and if I'd only wear makeup. I've heard it all before."

"But do look at Dickens!" Maggie said. "Have you ever seen a more beautiful dog?"

Everything always came back to Dickens.

REGINALD WROTE THEM a note that they found, handwritten and hand-delivered, sticking through the mail slot.

Dear Professor and Mrs. Holliss,

I would like to invite you to dinner to thank you for your great kindness. At a time that is convenient for you. This Sunday would be ideal, but any Saturday or Sunday evening this year would be fine. Shall we say this coming Sunday, at 7 pm?

> *Gratefully,*
> *Reginald Parker*

Claire was curious. "Who's this Reginald Parker?" she asked. "With a handwritten note, no less. Nobody writes by hand anymore. And why is he grateful?"

Maggie and David exchanged a meaningless look. She had not yet told him about the two-hundred-dollar loan and he had not told her about the picnic hamper of goodies.

"He saved the dog," David said.

"He saved Dickens," Maggie said.

"So why is he grateful?"

"I drove him home. He was nearly killed jumping in front of the truck to save Dickens. I bandaged his hands and drove him home."

"And for this he wants to have you to dinner?"

"How do we get out of this?" David said.

"Dear God," Maggie said.

"God has nothing to do with this. Think of a way out."

"Why not just go? It might be fun," Claire said. "Tell him I'm visiting and maybe he'll invite me as well."

"We could tell him Claire is visiting and so we can't come . . . go. Is that plausible?"

"But he says any Saturday or Sunday this year."

"This *year*!"

"At least he has a sense of humor." This was Claire. "He leaves you no way out." Claire laughed and they both turned to look at her since she was not given to laughter.

In the end they decided to get it over with as soon as possible. They accepted and Claire was invited along with them.

3.

Reginald met them at the door of the little cottage looking confused rather than welcoming, as if he hadn't really expected them to show up. Maggie and David introduced him to Claire and at once Claire and Reginald faced off.

"Welcome," Reginald said. He smiled.

"A pleasure," Claire said.

"Call me Reg," he said.

Claire made an instant assessment. She guessed he must be about forty-three, her own age. He was tall and skinny with sandy hair, balding in front, and a thin patchy beard. He was gazing at her with mild disappointment, as if he had expected someone younger and prettier. *You're no prize yourself*, she thought as she gave his hand a firm, manly squeeze. His looks were satisfying: he would be no challenge to her.

There was no telling what he thought of her.

"I love these guest cottages," Claire said.

"Reg," David said, and pressed on him the bottle of wine he had brought. "A modest merlot," he said, "with pretensions."

They all went inside. Suddenly a woman and child emerged

from the kitchen. The child was a girl of eight or nine, smiling shyly. The woman could have been any age, with her anxious face, pointed and foxy. They both had extraordinary red-gold hair pulled back in a ponytail and a trail of freckles across their noses. The mother looked thin to the point of malnutrition. She was smiling bravely but she appeared frightened.

"My wife, Helen," Reginald said, "and my daughter, Iris."

This was the first the Hollisses had heard of a wife and child.

They greeted each other carefully, except for Maggie, who suddenly lapsed into her old Sedgwick sociability.

"How nice!" she said. "We didn't know you existed. I mean, Reginald never mentioned a family and so we naturally thought . . . and what a pretty girl you are, Iris! Such lovely hair!"

Iris flushed with pleasure.

"Shall we sit down?" Maggie said, forgetting in her anxiety that she was not the hostess. "Well, what a nice surprise," she said. She looked from Helen to Iris and to the living room beyond.

The living room was small, with a dining table set up at one end and a desk and filing cabinet at the other. In the middle of the room two couches faced each other, a fireplace on the wall in between. The three Hollisses sat on one couch and faced the Parkers on the other. Reginald was still holding David's modest merlot.

"Lovely," Maggie said. "Cozy and lovely."

"We don't have a grand piano," Reginald said. "We don't have a swimming pool."

"Neither did we . . . once."

"But you do now."

"Well, yes."

"It must feel good to have everything."

"'There must be more to life than having everything.' Do you know that book by Sendak? It's absolutely delightful. *Higglety Pigglety Pop! or There Must Be More to Life*." She began to wonder if they had gotten the date wrong or if they had drifted by mistake into the wrong guest cottage. "This is a lovely room. And so nicely set up," Maggie said. "So." It was up to someone else now.

"I have to see to the dinner," Helen said. "Come with me, Iris."

"The boss has spoken," Reginald said. He got up and followed them into the kitchen.

Maggie poked David and whispered, "Good God!" He looked at her, shook his head, and said, "Don't."

Claire moved to the couch facing her parents. She was pleased with herself. She looked at her mother and father—Misery and Poop, just like the old days—and measured their growing discomfort. This was going to be an interesting evening.

"What can I get you to drink?" Reginald asked. He was leaning across the pass-through from the kitchen. "We can offer you tomato juice or orange juice or Calistoga water." He ducked his head back into the kitchen and a few seconds later joined them in the living room. "We don't drink here," he explained. "Not alcohol. So what would you like?"

They all decided on Calistoga water and Reginald disappeared again into the kitchen.

"This is gonna be one long night," David said.

"Shhh."

"What larks!" Claire said. "Tomato juice or orange juice or water!" She laughed happily.

Reginald returned with water for everyone. He seemed more relaxed now that he had drinks out of the way.

"Here's to the end of the Bush era," David said.

They raised their glasses toward one another.

"Alas," Reginald said, and no one followed up on that.

Claire let out a small giggle. "What larks!" she said.

Dickens first, and then the weather—unseasonably warm for Northern California—and then university gossip: this got them through the water aperitif and then it was time for dinner.

"THIS IS DELICIOUS," MAGGIE SAID. "What do you call it?"

They were eating an egg and avocado casserole with some green and red bits here and there, peppers and tomatoes. It was a concoction devised by Helen herself under the double pressures of economy and vegetarianism.

"It's just a thing I made," Helen said.

"Well, it's perfectly lovely," Maggie said. "Lucky you, Reginald. Reg. Have you been married long?"

Reginald and Helen exchanged glances and then Reginald said, "Just long enough to produce our lovely, obedient daughter."

Helen smiled. Suddenly she looked to be in her early twenties, remarkably fresh and pretty.

"And how did you meet?"

Helen began, "We met . . ."

"That's a long story," Reginald said in a way that made clear that he was not going to get into it and neither was Helen.

"Well?" Claire was not to be put off. "We've got all evening."

"Delicious," Maggie said. "You should be a chef, Helen." Inspired, she said, "We know Reginald is a novelist, but what do you do? Or are you a full-time mother?"

"I work at Walmart, part time."

"Walmart! How interesting! It's always in the news."

"For taking advantage of their part-time workers," Reginald said. "They keep you on a part-time schedule so they can deny you benefits. Health care, for example."

"And everyone needs health care," Maggie said, then there was a silence. "Something should be done."

"For the sake of justice," Claire said. She looked around but there were no takers. She nudged the subject forward with a little speech on the exploitation of women in communes by a patriarchy she likened to the Taliban but nobody responded and so she gave up and asked, "What grade are you in, Iris? You look very smart."

"I'm in fourth grade."

"She's supposed to be in third, but she skipped a grade," Reginald said. "But we don't praise her because we want to keep her humble."

"Why?" Claire said. It had an accusatory tone.

"To walk in the way of the Lord," he said. "Why else?"

"And how did he walk?"

"Humbly. Aware that he was God." He added, "And man."

"I've always wondered; if he was God, how could he be man?"

"It's the great Christian paradox," Reginald said.

"Yes, sure, but really?"

"What's so difficult to understand about paradox?"

Claire leaned forward to engage him. "Leave it," David said, and smiled at Helen and Reginald. "I'm afraid all the Hollisses are a bit deficient in the religion category."

"Speak for yourself," Claire said. "I almost became a nun."

Maggie sighed.

"A near miss," David said, and added, "for the nunnery."

"Poop!" Claire said, and Maggie said, "David!"

"Kidding. Just kidding."

"Tell us about being a nun. Or almost being one."

Claire went on at length about her interview with the Mother Superior, who had told her she had to be a Catholic before becoming a nun. And of course she had known that, Claire said, she was not an idiot, but she didn't want to become a Catholic before she was sure that becoming a nun was right for her. She wasn't about to plunge into another total commitment without some sense of how it fit her needs. She'd been through the commune business and the motherhood business and the lesbian business and this time she wanted to be certain before making a major commitment. She was sure he saw her point. Life was too short not to get the best. And she had decided religion was not the best.

She finished and looked to Reginald for some response but he seemed for the moment confused by her lengthy speech.

"How about opening that wine I brought," David said. He had reached the end of his patience with Claire's dreams of the good life or, in her case, the best. In the next moment she would be onto "give peace a chance."

"We don't drink," Reginald said.

"But we do," David said. "And I wouldn't want that wine to go to waste."

"The truth is we don't have a corkscrew."

"Yes, there's a kind of corkscrew thing on the side of that Swiss Army knife you've got," Helen said, and Reginald gave her a hard look. He got up and went out to the kitchen, where they could hear him rattling through the knives and forks in search of his Swiss Army knife.

"It's not too late for the wine?" Maggie asked.

"It's exactly the right time," David said.

"I'd love some wine," Iris said confidentially. "When I'm older."

Maggie smiled at her. Iris was a sweet child, and pretty. Why did they want her to walk in the way of the Lord? Why couldn't they all just have a good-night drink and go home?

"How're you doing out there, Reg?" Claire was invigorated by the likelihood of further conversation about her fling with the nunnery.

"These will have to do as wineglasses," Reginald said. He clutched three yellow juice glasses in one hand and the wine bottle in the other. He made a ceremony of pouring for David first and then for Maggie and Claire. In the yellow glasses the wine looked poisonous.

"I hope it's all right," he said.

"It's modest," David said, "with pretensions."

"Mmm," Maggie said.

Reginald sat down and cleared his throat. "This seems like the right moment to propose a toast." He raised his glass of Calistoga water. "To my friend Maggie in gratitude for the loan of money and to my friend David for his gift of food. Two perfect acts of Christian fraternity. Good health."

David drained his glass and refilled it. The others sipped decorously.

"Hear, hear!" Claire said. "Christian fraternity with the Hollisses!" She was delighted.

David and Maggie exchanged a look. They knew what Claire was up to—she loved to sabotage a party—but they did not know what to make of this new, Christian Reginald. And they were not at all happy at his revealing the loan and the picnic basket.

"Tell me," Claire said, "are you a born-again Christian? With Jesus as your personal savior and all that?"

"We're Christians. I wouldn't say we're extreme. We just believe in Christian values . . . like kindness, generosity, humility. We follow the Bible."

"So you believe in justice. Justice for part-time Walmart workers. Justice for immigrants, legal or illegal? Justice for gays and lesbians? Or do you only believe in justice for Christians, period?"

"We believe in the Bible and the brotherhood of Christians." He peered at Claire through his thick glasses. "I am my brother's keeper."

"Religion is so complicated," Maggie said.

"Life is complicated," Claire said. "Christianity is easy."

"Dear God," Maggie said.

Once again David filled their yellow glasses with wine.

"Back to the subject," Claire said. "When I almost became a nun, the Mother Superior I interviewed with was—like yourself, Reg—all excited about Christian virtues. Justice, I told her, is the one that matters. It pretty much includes all the others. But she wanted to insist on charity. Charity this. Charity that. And I said to her, 'Well, do you mean charity like giving to the Salvation Army and so forth or do you mean thinking nice thoughts about people, even when they're a pain in the behind?' She hemmed and hawed and it became evident that she meant both. From what she said I could see she had confused charity with faith. Now I realize I'm simplifying what is probably a complicated theological distinction—I'm not a theologian—but my point remains the same. Justice includes charity because charity has to be earned, it has to be deserved."

David had never heard such an exercise in sloppy thinking. He wondered for a wild moment if she really was their daughter. He had always held, sensibly, that all religions were dangerous but it was now clear to him that religion could make you crazy.

"So where does your notion of Christianity fit into this?" Claire asked.

"My works are Christian," Reginald said. "They're infused with Christianity."

"Your works. Like your novels, you mean?" Claire leaned forward, ready for him.

Reginald turned to David. "In your works, too, I always see the moral underpinnings of Christianity. In your *Thackeray* for instance. How are we to understand what you say about his loyalty to his crazy wife except in terms of Christian responsibility? Everything you say about Thackeray comes down to his fidelity or lack of fidelity to fundamental moral principles. It's a profoundly Christian book. And so is your book on Crane. Am I not right?"

David was stunned. He sipped his wine and tried to summon a response but before he could get his thoughts straight, Claire leaped in.

"Never mind him," Claire said. "What about you? I've never read any of your books—though I will, I promise—but are they born-again books? I mean, can you read them even if you're not a Christian?"

"My books are philosophical books rather than Christian per se." He leaned back, professorial, and adjusted his glasses. "I argue the great questions of life, like Mann and Proust and Murdoch. That may sound self-important but you have to remember that even the little people sometimes have deep thoughts."

"Well, shut my mouth!" Claire said. "Little people. Deep thoughts. You sound like somebody who was brought up on Sartre or Camus. 'The little people of Paris.' Jacques Brel is alive and well."

"Sartre and Camus are irrelevant to what I do. Your father knows what I'm talking about, don't you, David?"

"It's all too deep for me," David said. "I watch *Law and Order* on TV." The truth was that he watched *Judge Judy* but he felt safer in admitting to *Law and Order*.

"Could you pass the wine, Poop?"

David poured the last few drops of wine into Claire's juice glass.

"Well, this has been lovely," Maggie said, and shifted in her chair as if ready to go.

"But there's dessert," Helen said.

And so they sat through dessert—canned fruit cocktail—with more pointless, contrary talk between Claire and Reginald while despair settled over Maggie and David.

"Just lovely," Maggie said, and at last they were through the door and out into the cool, clean air of Northern California.

THEY WALKED HOME in silence, Maggie and David consumed with ancient notions of treachery and betrayal.

Claire, however, was exultant.

Claire had plans.

4.

The next day Claire and Reginald started their affair. It began briefly and messily, as if it were a minor skirmish before the real battle, and that is what it turned out to be.

They went to bed together in the early afternoon, while Helen was working at Walmart and Iris was at school, and after their brisk and feverish encounter Claire left Palo Alto for her planned reunion with Willow and her work at the antique lightboard for Willow's Baltimore New Repertory Theatre.

Claire and Reginald would not take up with each other again until more than a year had passed and the real battle had begun.

DAVID AND MAGGIE had a major quarrel on the night of the Parkers' dinner party, and the feeling of betrayal would continue to trouble each of them.

"I don't care about the money," David said. "It's not the money at all. It's the idea that he would ask you to loan him two hundred dollars and you wouldn't think to let me know about it. As if I might disapprove. It's as if the Sedgwick money was none of my business."

Maggie protested, as she always did at such times, that the Sedgwick money was theirs, not hers, and it was unfair of him after all these years to make that kind of accusation. What was the matter with him? Was he getting senile? Why, if you want to get picky about it, did he not mention the food basket he had sent to Reginald? Did he think the Holliss money had nothing to do with *her*? And on and on. Ancient rage. Ancient betrayal.

"It's not the same."

"It *is* the same. It's the same. It's the same. It's the same."

Blah, blah, blah.

Dickens, depressed, curled up under the kitchen table, where he was out of the way but available, if called upon, to help change the mood.

The quarrel went on for a good part of the night.

BY NOON THE NEXT DAY, when their rage had cooled and they had accepted the small duplicities each was guilty of, Maggie and David settled down to discuss the Parkers.

"What are we to make of the put-upon Helen?" Maggie said. "She seems catatonic, poor woman. Do you think she's aware that he's a fake?"

"You think he's a fake? I do, too," David said. "All that crap about the great questions of life and even little people having deep thoughts. What kind of novel can that mentality produce?"

"Does he even have a job? Does he teach? How do they manage to live?"

"And *she's* working at Walmart."

They began to deflect their anger at each other onto Walmart and the unworthy Reginald Parker.

"Have you ever been to Walmart?" David offered this in the interest of truth. "It's wonderful."

"When were you in Walmart?"

"Ages ago. I used to go there sometimes after I had my stroke, the first one, and get over-the-counter sleeping pills. They have fantastic bargains."

"Well, it's one thing to go there and another to have to work there."

"She has no health benefits."

"How do they live?"

"Maybe he's inherited money. Some people do."

Maggie gave him a suspicious look.

"I'm just saying."

"The child is sweet. Iris. Though she looks as put-upon as the catatonic mother. I don't know how women allow this kind of thing to happen to them. It's bad enough to be a faculty wife, where it's presumed your opinions are really your husband's and you're lucky to be married to an intellectual powerhouse. But to have to work at Walmart to support your husband while he goes for morning walks and pretends to write novels in the afternoon and, for all I know, sleeps around indiscriminately, well, I think that's just intolerable."

"It is. Intolerable."

Thus, by slow increments, they healed their marital rift.

MAGGIE WAS FOND OF presenting herself as a faculty spouse, that unacknowledged, abused species. This was a flaw in her character and she sometimes reflected on what it said about her. In her wilder moments she compared herself to the ballet dancer who, among her closest friends, exhibits her crushed toes and her cruelly malformed feet, proof of her dedication to art. But this, she recognized, was self-dramatization and not true of her at all. Being a faculty spouse was not high art—no White Swan for her—nor had she sacrificed herself in playing the role of wife. In fact she enjoyed it, and it came easily to her, since like so many other faculty spouses she was more naturally intelligent and more socially aware than her husband.

Maggie had been lucky in inheriting money and lucky again in her choice of husband. The troubles that came along with occasional ill health were made easier by having money in the bank, and the troubles that came along with three independent and unruly children were made manageable by a husband whose natural authority they respected. Moreover he was a university professor at a time when that still meant something and his position helped their kids out of the jams they repeatedly got themselves into. Maggie, then, was left free to be—as she was convinced she was—the loving, understanding, and always dependable mom. This was one of the few things about herself in which she was deceived. Her dependability varied with the needs of her husband. She was—and had more than once shown herself to be—capable of loving her children and ignoring them at the same time.

Dealing with an English faculty at a major university, Maggie had developed a keen eye for hypocrisy and an infallible ear for self-delusion. Thus she was aware that she wanted people to know she was a Sedgwick—she owed that much to the family—but at the same time she wanted them to realize that being a Sedgwick didn't matter to her at all. In the same way she was able to register the degrees of imbalance in the Parker family and, with a clarity of vision that would have disconcerted a lesser woman, in her own family as well.

For Maggie the Parkers presented a simple case of love and dependence. Helen loved Reginald to the exclusion of her own needs, and Reginald loved Reginald. Helen saw him as her superior in every respect. She felt fortunate to have been chosen by him to be the mother of his children and the provider of family security. He loved Helen, Maggie supposed, in his way. Iris, too, was drawn into this unquestioning worship of Reginald and it was undoubtedly in his own interest that he kept them walking in the way of the Lord. Reginald himself remained something of a mystery. Was it possible that he had some of the abundant talent that he felt justified in both his devotion to his art and his lack of interest in gainful labor? And then, too, there was the surprising boldness and generosity of his throwing himself in front of the UPS truck to save Dickens. A man who would do that for a stranger's dog could not be altogether bad. He was selfish, no doubt, but not bad. Thus far her reading of the Parker Situation.

Maggie knew selfishness when she saw it, even and especially in her own family. She worried often about Claire and her irresponsibility in abandoning her son Gaius to the Oregon commune and then later expecting Maggie and David to pay for his very expensive Princeton education. Maggie had no idea what Claire's life with Willow had been like but she imagined it had foundered on the rock of the usual: Claire comes first and good luck to whoever comes after. And now they were back together again. Did anyone ever learn anything? Claire maintained that she was a lesbian by choice because, quite simply, she had never had a good relationship with a man or a bad one with a woman. Perhaps Claire was not a real, committed lesbian. Now that Maggie thought of it, Claire showed every sign of being sexually attracted to Reginald Parker. All that hostility, that visceral need for confrontation. Maggie would worry about her if that dinner performance had been something new, but she had seen it all before and she was convinced that anyone as innocently selfish as Claire could not be hurt. Claire was indestructible. If a romantic encounter with Claire and Reginald should ever occur, Maggie figured, Reginald was the one who would come to grief.

Where, as a matter of fact, had Claire gone this afternoon?

Maggie turned these thoughts over in her mind as she brushed Dickens's coat to a lustrous shine. *Selfishness*, she said to herself, and thought of Sedge and Will. She wondered if, in her unquestioned devotion to David, she was the most selfish of them all. And what about her pride in being a Sedgwick? What nonsense. She was walking in the way of the Lord. Well, stumbling.

"Good boy," she said, and gave Dickens a gentle smack on his rump. "Time for walkies!"

MAGGIE AND DAVID drove Claire to the airport, each of them in varying states of good humor. Claire was in excellent spirits, full of talk about what fun the dinner with the Parkers had been and how lucky they were in their old age to have young friends, so unlike the old coots that Poop had taught with all these years. Reginald was interesting as a man, she said, even though she doubted he was an interesting novelist. And Helen was interesting, too, an anomaly really, since she was a faculty spouse—a nonperson—without actually being married to a professor. And the child, Iris, was adorable. Claire shifted in her seat with excitement. She couldn't wait to read *What Is Not Being Said*, though she doubted if it would ever be published in her lifetime. But she liked the idea of it.

Listening to her daughter go on this way, Maggie concluded, *Yes, God help us all, Claire has gone to bed with Reginald Parker.* She was relieved to drop her off at the San Francisco airport with their customary goodbyes.

"Love you, Misery. Love you, Poop."

"Love you," David said.

"Love you," Maggie said.

"She is now in the hands of Weeping Willow," Maggie said to David, and was ashamed to find herself thinking, *And good riddance, good riddance.*

CLAIRE WENT TO the little cocktail lounge for a glass of wine while she waited for her flight and, to make the time go by, she tipped open her laptop intending to see what Wikipedia had to say about Iris Murdoch. She was annoyed to see the little pig with a letter in its mouth reminding her that she had mail. *Willow*, she thought, and stuck out her square jaw. *This had better not be trouble.* She was surprised, and surprisingly pleased, to see it was a note from Reginald Parker. It was brief and unsigned.

> Thinking of you, Chiara, as I try to concentrate on my novel of ideas. I have a few ideas of my own. You?

Claire smiled. He had remembered her story about being born in Italy and misnamed Chiara. Was he one of those men who actually listen? Even in bed? She fired back a note at once.

> Dear Reg: All men are pigs. Claire.

She thought about the message for a minute or two, wondering if he might take it the wrong way, and decided to sign off not as Claire but as Chiara. She hit the Send button. What larks! This might be the start of an affair. She felt not the least twinge of guilt. She couldn't wait to tell Willow.

But Reg sent her a second email while she sat there with her wine. She had not closed her laptop. Was she hoping he would respond, and at once?

Cara Chiara: You are absolutely right about men, as you
are about everything. It has been an honour (spelling sic;
I favour the British spelling) to sport with you in my sty,
even though the memory keeps me from work on my novel.
Yours, Reg.

Claire lingered over this. She still had twenty minutes before
boarding time, and it was tempting to respond. She was surprised once again at how pleased she was to be courted, even
mock-courted if that's what was going on. *Was it mockery?* she
wondered. This was an unworthy thought and it merely flick-
ered across her brain and she dismissed it at once. After all, he
had confided to her at length about his novel. Such sincerity
canceled out any chance of mockery. She sipped the last of her
wine and made her decision.

Sir, you are a married man and you're writing to a woman
who was almost a nun. How do you reconcile your behavior
with walking in the way of the Lord?

She looked at this message for a while, considering its tone
and what Reginald might make of it and decided, *What the hell*,
and sent it. Unsigned.

She left the lounge and went to catch her flight, feeling un-
usually attractive.

Reginald had left several emails on her laptop by the time she
reached Baltimore but by then she was in Willow territory and
she ignored them. He was a married man and she was here in

Baltimore to give another try at building a life with Willow. What she wanted out of this life was a relationship like Misery and Poop's, but when she considered their marriage in all its aspects she realized it required a selfishness she was not sure she had in her.

Meanwhile Reginald continued to write her friendly, noncommittal, and occasionally obscene emails. It would be only a matter of a week before they became fervent correspondents.

5.

Maggie and David gradually recovered from the dinner party and, less gradually, from the damages of Claire's visit.

"It really was the dinner from hell," Maggie said. "Why did he invite us in the first place?" This was three days after the party.

"Because you gave him money," David said.

"Loaned."

"*Loaned* him money. And because I, like an idiot, sent a lavish picnic basket to a man who doesn't drink. Charles Heidsieck 1995!"

"It's not right."

"Hold that thought."

"I suspect he smokes. I ran into him once with Dickens and he seemed high to me. Like Sedge in the old days."

"I could have sent him marijuana for a lot less than I paid for that damned food basket. Charles Heidsieck!"

"I've never felt so unwelcome anywhere."

"I didn't want to go in the first place."

"Well, it's in the past now and we can forget about it."

"I've forgotten it already."

"I have, too. However . . ."

———

A WEEK AFTER the party they were out walking Dickens and of course they ran into Reginald. It was a cool, clear September day with the promise of a light breeze toward afternoon and the Hollisses were enjoying the California feeling that everything would turn out all right, even the stock market, even the wars in Iraq and Afghanistan.

"Dickens! My old doggy friend! How's this good boy? What a great old dog you are."

Dickens allowed himself to be scratched and pummeled. Dickens had been a puppy when Reginald first met him those years ago but he was getting on in age now and was more sedate about receiving homage.

"We've never thanked you for that lovely dinner party," Maggie said.

Reginald looked puzzled. "You sent us that beautiful note."

"But we haven't thanked you in person. Or your lovely wife. It was so lovely to meet her. And your lovely Iris."

"Well, you're welcome," Reginald said. "We must do it again, soon."

They were silent for a moment with nothing more to say.

At this point Dickens did his part by tugging at the leash.

"Off to the park," David said. "Dickens is getting impatient."

They said goodbye. As soon as they were a few feet away, David said to Maggie, "Promise me, promise me now and forever, that there will be no return engagement for that dinner!"

"He was just being polite."

"Never again."

"We can wait for weeks. Even a month. Before we have them back."

"I'll divorce you. I swear to God I will."

"God?"

"I swear I will."

TWO WEEKS WENT by and they had finally stopped talking about the dinner. Claire's visit, however, remained very much with them. It was getting close to Claire's birthday and they would have to send her the usual check.

"Why does she hate us?" Maggie said, not really expecting an answer.

"She doesn't hate us. She hates you."

"That's what I meant."

"Poor old thing. Don't take it so hard. Nobody sane could possibly hate you." He put his arm around her and gave her a peck on the cheek. "She's just a tad crazy."

"Is that the answer, then? We've made her crazy?"

"Look at her life. The causes, the commune, poor little Gaius"—it was still hard for him to use the name of Claire's baby—"not to mention the lesbian alliance with Weeping Willow." He paused for a moment when he saw tears coming. "Don't," he said, "don't cry. You've done everything you could." And then, when he felt sure the tears had passed, he said, "Do you think the lesbian phase caused the interest in religion? Or vice versa?"

But the tears had not passed and, still weepy, she said, "Can you just see her as a nun!"

"The righteousness." He pulled himself up and made a righteous face. "Fighting for justice against charity."

"She's a terrorist," Maggie said in the easy parlance of that day.

"A domestic terrorist," David said. "And none the less scary for that."

REGINALD HAD TEA ready for Helen when she returned from Walmart. It was one of the things she enjoyed most about life with Reginald: he would sometimes surprise her like this. Earl Grey was steeping in the pot and he had placed miniature éclairs on a china plate and he greeted her at the door with an embrace that reassured her that Walmart was behind her and she was safely, warmly, home.

Writing was his life, he always said, and his day built up to and away from those hours at the computer. Moreover he was aware that those hours were made possible by Helen's willingness to sacrifice herself at Walmart, and so preparing her tea and making a small fuss about every month or so seemed to him an equitable trade-off.

Over time Reginald had become sincerely devoted to Helen and it was a fact they both accepted that she was simply unable to meet all of his needs. But that was not surprising. Reginald was an intellectual with secrets of the mind and heart that he must keep for his writing. It was a rare person with whom he could share that part of himself out of which he created and it was Helen's ill luck that he found that rare person in Claire. Helen, as a matter of religion, never inquired about Reginald's writing—his privacy was sacred to her—nor did she so much as glance at his computer. If she had, she might have found his cache of emails to and from Claire, the first of them dated that Monday afternoon of messy and fevered lovemaking.

Implicitly Helen understood that what she did not know could not hurt her.

"I'VE DECIDED I CAN'T DO IT," Maggie said.

A month had passed since the ghastly evening at the Parkers' and still she had not worked up the courage to invite them to dinner.

"Can't do what?" David asked. He was sitting at the kitchen table with his battered copy of *The Odd Women* waiting for his cup of tea.

"Can't invite Reginald to dinner."

"Thank you and thank you and thank you. You are the love of my life. You make the sun come up. You are Venus and Athena and Diana rolled into one. You are wisdom incarnate. If there were a God, she would be you."

"It's not the work. It's the agony of the conversation. Because without Claire, we'd have to talk about personalities or books. And the Parkers don't have personalities, any of them except maybe little Iris, and if we talk about books, they'll ask you about your work on Gissing and you'll have a hissy fit and it will be the dinner party from hell all over again."

David considered objecting to "hissy fit" but saw that the best outcome of this exchange lay in confirming her decision not to invite them to dinner. Period. "That's it," he said. "*C'est ça. E giusto. Certum'st.*"

"*Certum'st?*"

"Latin. Silver age. Plautus."

"You're such a smart man!" She poured him his tea then and he was perfectly content that the matter was settled at last, and peacefully, too.

And so the next morning David was dumbfounded and dismayed when they encountered Reginald on their walk and, to cover a momentary silence, Maggie said, "We must have you and Helen to dinner one of these days."

BUT BEFORE ANY DATE could be found to invite the Parkers to dinner, an email came from Iris asking—on behalf of her father—for a loan of four hundred dollars. It was urgent and embarrassing, she wrote, but her father promised to repay them in full and promptly. She signed the email, "Your Friend, Iris."

PART TWO

❖ ❖ ❖

6.

A terrorist from Nigeria was arrested on Northwest Airlines with a bomb in his underwear, a Christmas surprise. The panic level went to bright orange. Fortunately the FBI and the CIA were keeping the homeland safe for lesser, domestic terrorists. It was 2009 and health care was the big political issue and the Tea Party was saying no.

Meanwhile, at the house of Maggie and David, the sum of all issues foreign and domestic was Iris's request for a loan.

BUT IRIS HERSELF was a dear. You could not—you must not—confuse Iris with her father. She was only doing what he wanted her to do. What he insisted she must do. And so she did it. That's what was so offensive. The coercion of a minor. No child takes it upon herself to write an email requesting a loan of four hundred dollars. It was preposterous. It was horrible. But Iris herself was a dear. You could not blame Iris, the poor thing. Or that mother, Helen. Two innocent women taken advantage of by a cold, lazy, calculating malingerer. Are we making too much of this?

So went the discussion of Iris's request for a loan, Maggie and David outdoing each other in mild, rather good-natured indignation.

And then there was the swing back to sweet reasonableness.

What after all is four hundred dollars? Either of them would immediately write a check for four hundred dollars to Second Harvest or to the Alzheimer's fund or to those nice people at the Southern Poverty Law Center who were always going after racists and anti-Semites and whatever new bigots appeared in the land, the Muslim haters most recently. The Hollisses recognized their duty as citizens and academics to pay taxes and support worthy charities.

And God knows—Maggie insisted—they had squandered as much and a great deal more as patrons of the opera and the symphony and the Stanford art museum. Not to mention what went out on birthdays to the three grandkids in England and don't forget the Princeton wonder, Gaius, now joyously employed. That tuition! Four hundred dollars? They had put down a hundred thousand on houses for Sedge and Will and, during the post-commune, early-Willow period, for Claire as well.

To be fair, those hundred thousands were taken from stocks at a time in the eighties and nineties when the market was singing a heroic tune—they had added a good million or more to their portfolio—and so the Hollisses suffered no permanent damage to their initial two million. At least not then. They had lost some thirty percent, however, in the disasters of 2008 and 2009 and recovered very little of it since, so they weren't flush anymore. Not really. Not flush enough to be giving away four hundred dollars. To strangers.

But for that matter the Southern Poverty Law people were strangers, weren't they? To be honest? And the Alzheimer's people? And Second Harvest?

Oh, God—Maggie again—sometimes it was impossible to think clearly. And suddenly, for no reason whatsoever, it came to her that this was all Claire's fault. Which made no sense, really, and she was ashamed of herself. No wonder Claire hated her so. But—she tried again—the money was not the point. It was the borrowing that was the point. It was the fact of being asked, and asked in this outrageous way, that made the request so offensive. Using the child, Iris. Isn't that it? Isn't that right?

Yes, the request was offensive and having Iris do the asking made it doubly offensive, but what bothered David most of all was the intrusion into their privacy. Asking for the loan of money was an intimate act. It depended on a level of trust and affection and, well, intimacy. An intimacy, he was happy to say, that simply did not exist. And would never exist between the Hollisses and the Parkers.

Why not just write him the goddam check and have done with it?

But David was caught up in his intimacy theory and spent some time developing it. He didn't appreciate unasked-for intimacy any more than he appreciated talk about religion. And on. And on. When he was done, he poured himself a drink and sat back, satisfied and a little embarrassed.

"Well, what shall we do?" he said. "I'm fed up with thinking about it."

"I'm getting one of my headaches."

"Maybe we're making too much out of this."

"After all, it's only four hundred dollars."

"Why not just write him the check and have done with it?"

"Good idea."

"You write it and sign it from both of us."

"What a lot of fuss."

"Over nothing. Still . . ."

7.

My sense of obligation is all that holds this family together, Maggie said to herself. She had decided not to say it to David even though it was true. Perhaps *because* it was true. She was thinking of her children and how disappointing they had all turned out, except for Will, who was the perfect son. But he had moved to another country, probably to get away from them. Still she was determined to love them as David loved them, though she secretly suspected that he, too, was exasperated at the fecklessness of Sedge and the mindlessness of Claire and the isolation of Will's family in Essex. Well, she was obliged to love them and so she did.

"We love them because we're obliged to," she said to David. He was undressing for bed and was sucking in his belly to conceal how much weight he was putting on.

"And because we're guilty. Of having so much and having each other," he said.

"Stop holding your breath like that," she said. "You'll injure yourself. Anyhow, I quite like your new rolls of flesh. They make me feel less bad about my own advancing decrepitude."

"It's all guilt," he said. "Life is."

"And a sense of obligation," she said.

DAVID WAS NOT EASILY persuaded of anything except by the exercise of his own good powers of reason and, in most other cases, by Maggie. All that fuss about the loan of four hundred dollars was the effect of being a scholarship student who married a woman with two million dollars. You had to remember that there was a time in America, even in California, when a woman with two million dollars was thought to be rich. Oh, the guilt of having so much.

Maggie did not look particularly rich when David first met her, perhaps because she hadn't yet come into Aunt Sedgwick's trust fund, and so it was a pleasant surprise—and in some ways dismaying—to discover that they could bypass graduate student housing and live in apartments like their professors. Their money made for comfort and the efficient use of study time since they didn't have to teach freshman comp to pay the rent, and by the time they had their first child they were able to afford a full-time nanny. The dismaying aspect was their distance from the problems and needs of other graduate students. They were largely alone, with the two other couples who also came from money. These were friendships of convenience that did not outlast the drive toward the PhD, and Maggie and David were from the start thrown largely upon each other. They found this sufficient, but for David in particular there was always the nagging fear that Maggie's money left them isolated and more dependent on each other than was good. He came very quickly to resent her money.

Maggie's money made it possible for them to finish their obligatory coursework in only two years and to write their PhD dissertations in three, and so David's resentment of her money was unfair, unreasonable, and the source of all their early quarrels. Nonetheless when David was offered a job as an assistant professor at Stanford, it was naturally assumed that Maggie would accompany him and teach the odd course in freshman comp when and if there was a course open. It was the 1960s and that's how things were then, that's how lives were disposed.

They bought a house in Old Palo Alto with four bedrooms and three baths—they had two boys by now—with a study for David and a grand piano for Maggie so she could keep up her playing while she waited for that call asking her to teach freshman comp. They were not quite unique among assistant professors in being able to buy a house. There were still a few of those odd sons of rich families who felt it a duty to teach for one dollar a year, and one of these—Gene Stockman—was an assistant professor in the English department. He was smart and funny and, best of all, he was still single and therefore useful as the odd man at dinner parties. In the campus revolutions of the late '60s, however, he heard the call of social justice and left to marry an African American woman and teach at Howard University. The Hollisses were left alone with their grand piano and their guilt.

Worse than the guilt was the insecurity it inspired, an insecurity that carried over from David's marriage into his professional life. He doubted he would ever get tenure because he seemed unable to turn his doctoral dissertation on Thackeray into the published book required for tenure. This was especially hurtful since Maggie's dissertation on Charlotte Brontë had been published—with almost no revision—by the University of Chicago Press. Since then she had come to regard scholarship as a thing of the past, at least for her, something she had tried, succeeded at, and then given up to be a faculty wife. But David was not able to give up and he felt unable to go on.

"Just do a page a day," Maggie said. "Take Saturday and Sunday off."

He was persuaded by this—after all, it had worked for her—and found that, once he got rid of all the excess filler proper to a dissertation, there remained a nice sturdy core of research he was able slowly, so slowly, to turn into an acceptable academic study. He did his page a day and finished the book in his sixth year and got tenure in an unremarkable seventh. It was pointed out to him by an unhappy chairman that most assistant professors earned tenure a year earlier. Nonetheless they were happy to welcome him—and his lovely wife and children—as permanent members of the department family.

Fuck you, David thought, but he said only that he was pleased and honored, and so were his lovely wife and children.

That evening over drinks, a little downcast, he told Maggie what the chairman had said.

"And what did you say?"

"I said, 'Fuck you and thanks very much.'"

"No, not really."

"Really. I did. 'Fuck you,' I said." But later that night before they fell asleep he said, "I didn't really say it. I just thought it."

"I was glad you said it," Maggie said. "And I'm glad that you didn't say it. But what I'm really glad about is that you told me the truth. I have the failed academic's preference for the truth." And then they made love.

Making love was very fine, of course, but afterward there was reality to face. David was convinced it was Maggie's money that was the problem. The department chair didn't have any; he lived in a cheap condo in the poor people's section of Palo Alto on the far side of El Camino and it gratified him to make life difficult for somebody like David who always had things easy.

It was a common enough attitude. It was probably Reginald Parker's attitude. And why not? From Reginald's point of view David had nothing to feel guilty about except being rich. But in fact David had enough guilt for both of them. Moreover his guilt affected everything he did and everything he thought. It was why, in exasperation, he had said, "Why not just write him the goddam check and have done with it!"

And so Maggie had written the check and signed it from both of them and popped it in the mail. It was the right thing to do. And to hell with the money.

A WEEK PASSED and then another and then one Saturday morning Reginald Parker appeared at their front door with Iris by his side. Dickens snuffled his way through the partly open door and nuzzled Reginald for a pat and then gave licks to Iris. It was a full doggy welcome and it broke the tension.

"I have to apologize," Reginald said. He shifted from one foot to the other while Iris concentrated on petting Dickens. It was clear that the child was embarrassed.

"We were about to walk Dickens," Maggie said, just to say something, though she and David had only now returned from the dog park. "Iris, you're looking so lovely with that red-gold hair."

Iris smiled in response.

"I'm afraid I owe you an apology," Reginald said, and he held out a small white envelope bulging with money. "I wouldn't want you to get the wrong idea. The truth is that I borrowed money from you that time when I was in a financial bind—could I come in for a moment? It's embarrassing to be talking about money out on the front step—but I don't want you to think I make a habit of it." They all moved indoors and were standing awkwardly in the foyer, where David joined them to see what was going on. Reginald still held the envelope in his hand. "Anyhow, I wasn't the one who asked for this loan, although I did need the money. It was my sweet little Iris. She heard me saying to Helen that I was in a bind and she knew you had loaned me money before and so she wrote that email all on her own. Didn't you, Iris?" He sounded almost proud of her.

Iris nodded her head yes and continued to study the floor.

"So, here's the money and I apologize for my daughter." He extended the envelope to Maggie and said, "You can count it, if you want. I guarantee it's all there."

Maggie shook her head no. "I'm sure it's fine," she said.

"What do you say, Iris?"

"I wrote the email," Iris said, and flushed crimson.

Maggie thought, *He's making her lie.*

And David thought, *Is there no end to this humiliation?*

"Well, I'm glad that's over and we're all square again. I hate borrowing from friends."

"Time for walkies," Maggie said and Dickens responded eagerly. Maggie laid the envelope on a side table and, almost casually, ushered everybody out of the house and down the front path. Reginald and Iris said goodbye and, tired as they were, Maggie and David set out for a second morning walk. At the end of the street, seeing the Parkers were safely out of sight, they turned back and slipped into their front door as if they were thieves.

For the next three days the white envelope lay on the side table in the foyer. Neither of them touched it. Neither of them wanted to count the money. When Maggie did finally open the envelope, she was not altogether surprised to find it contained two hundred rather than the four hundred dollars Reginald had borrowed. She knew she should mention this to David but she did not have the courage.

Besides, it was worth two hundred dollars just to have all this over with.

8.

Willow was now director of the New Repertory Theatre in Baltimore and so when Claire abandoned the commune and took up again with Willow, she offered herself as the house lighting expert. Willow accepted. The theater itself had been sitting idle for many years and, even refurbished, it still suffered from an ancient electrical system, with a lightboard and a network of overhead grids that required gels and filters and an agile young person on a long ladder to make the lighting work properly. Nonetheless Claire took to this old-fashioned theater works as if she had at last found her true vocation. She seemed to have an innate sense of how a red filter or a bank of soft yellows would add to an actor's appeal from the fourth row and sustain that appeal to the fourteenth. She had studied lighting in her senior year at Columbia, but seeing that it had no natural or useful function in any social movement, she had abandoned the artifice of theater for the hard realities of the commune. It was only a matter of months—and after the birth of Gaius—before she discovered the abundance of artifice in the emotional life of the commune. Authenticity was what she wanted and she found that in theater. She would work her social magic by bringing the harsh realities of life to the unwilling attention of theatergoers while she herself huddled in the delicate embrace of Willow.

Like Claire, Willow was the daughter of privilege. Her family had at first been appalled when she announced she was a lesbian but then, after her brief fling with suicide, they not only accepted her as she was but supplied her with endless credit to set up and manage and finally to direct her own New Repertory Theatre. They became her most generous theater patrons as well as the most enthusiastic supporters of whatever lover drifted into and then out of her life. Willow, they were surprised to discover, was not easy for other people to love. She was beautiful in her way, aristocratically long-faced and hardscrabble thin, with a pale, pale complexion. Like Claire, she wore no makeup. Also like Claire, she was manipulative by nature. She was demanding and devious. She needed solitude as much as she needed love. Few lovers met her needs and thus far only Claire had demonstrated any staying power. Willow's parents liked Claire for her self-proclaimed honesty and for her ability to keep Willow interested and alive. They supported Willow and Willow supported Claire.

When Claire arrived back in Baltimore the theater was in the final weeks of rehearsal of Albee's *The American Dream*. The aging actress playing Grandma—seized by a sudden excess of exhilaration—flung herself into the arms of the Van Man who had come to whisk her away to the Home, and when he failed to catch her, she fell to the stage floor and broke her arm. She was determined to go on, but the injury to her arm seemed strangely to have affected her memory and she dropped out of rehearsal and out of the performance. Claire went on for her. She was a quick study and the part—with its mixture of eccentricity and sentimental honesty—fitted her perfectly. She got up the lines in two days flat but there was a bad moment when they discovered she was unable to move naturally onstage. This problem was solved by Willow, who offered her refuge in a La-Z-Boy lounger, where her arms and hands could substitute for the business of acting. Claire sank gratefully into the chair and deliriously into the role and by the first performance she felt like Maggie Smith. Indeed, she played the part in the manner of an aged Maggie Smith, as was noted by two of the three reviewers of the play. "Artifice at its peak," the first reviewer said. "Old age has never seemed so witty and attractive." The second reviewer praised "her ability to take affectation beyond acting and into the exquisite air of truth." She got laughs for every other line and at the curtain call she was awarded what passed for a standing ovation.

As a matter of fact, Albee's Grandma was a role in which it was nearly impossible to fail, and informed by Claire's mimicry of long-gone Grandma Sedgwick, her performance had a convincing cutting edge. She was, for the moment, a star.

The reviews went straight to Claire's head and she determined that since she was now an actress, she must take steps to learn something about acting. She hired a voice coach and enrolled in an acting class with a once-famous Broadway actress and twice a week she took the train from Baltimore to New York to learn the elements of her craft. She was astonished to find she was an artist and concluded that all the turmoil of her earlier life proceeded from this: she had been living with an artist's temperament but without the platform for truth and violence provided by art. Henceforth, she resolved, her fierce integrity would be dedicated to the theater.

Willow was delighted at Claire's triumph as Grandma but not so delighted at what this meant to their relationship. Claire remained the truth teller she had been even before the commune, but now her pronouncements often came in a trained voice that made the truth sound rehearsed. And at odd moments there was a kind of grandeur to Claire that may not have been new but certainly was annoying. "Will you hand me that book," as she lay sprawled bulkily on the couch, came to sound eerily like Cleopatra's "I have immortal longings," or so it seemed to the theater director's mind of Willow as she delivered the requested book. And had Claire become less emotionally dependent, Willow wondered, or did she just seem that way?

Whatever the case, when Claire told Willow she would need a good deal more money to meet the cost of becoming an actress, Willow—in her solitary mood—responded that the economy was in a recession, that the cost of running the theater was crippling, that box office receipts could not be depended upon, that Claire was being overcharged by her speech coach, not to mention the cost of that Broadway has-been, and as a matter of fact . . .

"Fuck all that," Claire said, "I'll ask Poop. I'll ask Misery."

Thus in early November Maggie and David received an anniversary card accompanied by the reviews of Claire's performance as Grandma and a request for seven thousand dollars to pursue the study and practice of her art.

"Just take it out of my share of the inheritance," Claire wrote.

"LOOK AT THIS," MAGGIE SAID. "She's an actress all of a sudden."

Maggie read the reviews aloud to David and, despite their initial skepticism, they were both impressed. They looked at each other, hopeful.

"Wouldn't it be wonderful if she found something that made her happy," Maggie said. "Maybe she can be an actress. Do you think she can be an actress?"

"She's smart enough," David said, "and it's not as if she plans on becoming Meryl Streep. She just wants to study—what does she say?—'study and practice her art.'" He turned that over in his mind. "Hmm. 'Her art.' Do I hear Ds of G?"

"Delusions of Grandeur are fine so long as she's happy."

"It would be wonderful for her."

"And for us."

"And we owe it to her."

Maggie looked again at the reviews. She reread the letter.

"'Just take it out of my share of the inheritance.' I like that. She thinks we're her bankers."

"It's only Will who never asks for money."

WILL SENT HIS OWN usual anniversary card and enclosed a picture of himself and his wife and their three beautiful daughters. Maggie opened the card as they were having mid-morning coffee.

"Now look at this," Maggie said. "This is what I call a family. They're beautiful and intelligent—you can just tell—and they're happy. Will has always been the perfect son."

"The Perfect Son," David said, "in capital letters."

Then Maggie read aloud the accompanying letter.

Dear Mother and Father:

We're having an early winter here in Essex, both outside and inside. That is, an uncommon coldness has descended on us early and, I fear, fatally, in the country, the city, and, alas, in our lovely home, the home you both so generously helped me and Daphne to acquire. Do not fear, all is well with Daphne and the girls; it is I who am discomfortable. To be brief, I have decided to move on with my life, not from my teaching position here at Essex nor from Essex ipse but from my marriage to Daphne and from the lovely home aforementioned. Though I risk becoming that sad academic cliché—the middle-aged professor with the graduate student wife—I have chosen as my new partner in life Cloris Sears, a participant in my Yeats seminar. Cloris is young, true, but

extraordinarily mature for her age (twenty-six) and
does not seem to mind my being almost twice her age
or my momentary encumbrance with wife and family.
(Divorce takes time in England.) I know that you, as the
devoted parents you have always been, will continue to wish
me well and will maintain a familial relationship with
Daph and the girls and I hope you will understand that at
this time what I need, in addition to your customary
empathy, is the loan (against my inheritance, please) of fifty
thousand dollars for a down payment on a cottage for me
and Cloris. These are difficult times financially for everyone
and thus I particularly appreciate having parents who have
always been ready to help their grateful children.

You will be interested to know I have made great
progress on my study of Yeats's prosody. I investigate and
reject the early twentieth-century movement in science that
invented machines for measuring rhythm in the human
body and used their dubious discoveries to make further
claims about culture and race, specifically about the Irish. In
my study I will disprove the asserted relationship between
science and poetry and locate my new study of Yeats's prosody
in an analysis of ancient Celtic runes. This has been
attempted before now but I am working with newly
discovered texts and anticipate a great deal of scholarly
attention to this new work. I know you will be pleased to
hear this.

About the money: you can simply forward it to my bank;
you have the routing number from last time.

"And he wishes us much joy on our wedding anniversary," Maggie said. "That's it. That's the letter. From the Perfect Son."

David sat there, dumb, looking into his coffee.

"Damn it all to hell," Maggie said and tears rose to her eyes.

David got up and put his arms around her. He held her close until the tears stopped and then he said, "It's all right, sweet, everything will be all right. We'll still be able to see the grandkids and you know he'll look after Daphne. He'll get a divorce and he'll buy a little cottage for this new one, Clorox"—Maggie smiled or at least tried to—"and we'll bail him out when it's time for the next divorce. We've got plenty of money . . . as he cleverly notes . . . and we'll continue the running tab we have on all three of our wonderfully independent offspring. And cheer up. Just think of Claire. Poverty-loving, truth-telling Claire. She wants only seven thousand. We're the Rothschilds of the little people. Which—the little people—makes me think of Reginald Parker with his modest requests. How could we have begrudged him a few hundred dollars? How terrible we were. How irresponsible."

Maggie had so far recovered by now that she had an answer for him. "It wasn't the money itself with Reginald, it was the awkwardness of being asked for a loan from somebody who's essentially a stranger. When we give money to the kids, we know it's a gift, like it or not, and we don't expect to see it returned in our lifetime. With Reginald it's different. He's not our child, for one thing, and for another it's all too personal."

"Too intimate. Too intrusive. He's always been like that. Since we first met him he's forced his way into our lives. He's not honest."

Maggie thought of the two hundred dollars in the white envelope when there should have been four. She still hadn't told David. "Why do you say that?" she asked.

"Everything about him is dishonest. I pity that little girl."

"Which? The one he married or poor little Iris?"

"Both, though Iris was the one I had in mind. I wish there was something we could do for her without getting involved with the father."

"I'll think of something." She was thinking ahead.

"I'll divorce you, I swear to God."

"God?"

But he was in no mood to fool around with theology.

IT WAS, OF COURSE, in this same week that Sedge made his own request for a loan. This was a true loan since he had every intention of paying them back. He needed a quick hundred thousand for a down payment on a little house in the Hollywood Hills. The new location wasn't convenient to his research lab in downtown Los Angeles but it provided an escape from the smog and the chemical poisons of the city and the overabundance of available women. This new house had nothing to do with his most recent divorce—his fourth—except inasmuch as it was a guarantee that he would never risk marriage again. He was not meant for marriage. He was a born loner and would remain so forever. Now about that loan . . .

Maggie and David groaned, then laughed. This was the perfect anniversary remembrance.

"I'll call Michael Kelly," David said, referring to their accountant. "He'll pull the money chain."

"It's like Job," Maggie said. "Except we still have each other."

9.

t was a cold November day at the start of the rainy season and Maggie was dozing over her book. She was curled up uncomfortably in her little reclining chair, but at least she was officially reading and not taking a nap. David took naps. Since his last stroke—a mild one, a reminder of what could really happen one day—he had made a habit of putting on his pajamas and getting into bed for a good hour every afternoon. It did nothing for his disposition, since he often woke up groggy and impatient, but they both liked to believe it did something for his general health. Maggie preferred her unofficial nap in her reading chair.

The doorbell rang and she said, "Yes, yes," before she realized what was happening, and then she pushed herself out of her chair. The house was cozy. It was a shame to have to answer the door. Dickens raised his head from where he lay at her feet, considering whether he should follow her. It seemed necessary and so he did it, slowly.

Iris Parker stood on the doorstep, shy and brave.

"I'm sorry to bother you, Mrs. Holliss, but I wonder if you would let me take Dickens for a walk. My playdate has been canceled because Emma has a bad cold, and I can't go home until five, so I thought I could walk Dickens for you and use up the time."

The words came out all in a rush, as if she were reciting lines for a play.

"Come in, Iris, it's cold and damp out there."

Iris came inside and rubbed her hands together. "It's so nice and warm in here," she said. She patted Dickens, who had recognized Iris's voice.

"You're cold, Iris. Come into the kitchen with me and I'll make you some hot chocolate. My children always wanted hot chocolate on a winter day like this."

Iris followed her dutifully and sat at the kitchen table. Maggie went about pouring milk in a pan and mixing in the chocolate syrup.

"Of course it isn't really winter yet, is it. And besides, winter in California just means a lot of rain and a little cold. It's nothing like New England. I grew up in Connecticut and they have real winters there, with snow up to your waist sometimes." She looked over at Iris and saw that she seemed more at ease now. Dickens joined them in the kitchen and curled up at Iris's feet.

"Are you all right, Iris? You seemed upset when you rang the bell." Iris gave her a shy smile. "But I was half-asleep, reading my book, and so I may be, you know, mistaken. But it doesn't matter, does it. Tell me about your playdate. Emily has a bad cold?"

"Emma. Her mother wouldn't let her go to school and our playdate was canceled and I'm not expected home until five."

"What happens at five?"

"Five is when I can go home. That's when my dad's work is over."

"And what work is that?"

"His writing. He writes in the morning and he thinks and does research in the afternoon. He has to have private time."

"Private time, of course." Maggie turned this over in her mind. Private time doing what? Sorting through the big ideas while your own child waits outside in the cold? It was outrageous. And the rain. Though, to be honest, the rains hadn't begun yet.

"You should be wearing a sweater on a day like this, Iris."

"I have lots of sweaters. It wasn't cold when I left for school this morning."

"Do you have a raincoat and a rain hat?"

"I have everything," Iris said, and smiled broadly.

Maggie poured the hot chocolate into a large cup and brought it to the table with a plate of cat-tongue cookies.

"This is very nice," Iris said, "but truly I was not trying to ingratiate myself with you when I asked if I could walk Dickens. I really wanted to take Dickens for a walk. And use up the time. Until five."

Ingratiate. What an extraordinary child this was.

"Do you like school, Iris? Do you love to read?"

"I *love* to read. I've read almost all the Nancy Drews."

"And would you like to write your own books someday?"

In this way they used up the time until five, when Iris could at last go home.

A WEEK LATER Iris rang the bell again and once again David was in bed napping and Maggie was in her chair pretending not to. The winter rains had begun and it was good napping weather, but the doorbell rang and, like all things unpleasant in life, it had to be dealt with. Maggie opened the door to find Iris, wet and looking guilty. She stood there shivering in a pale blue raincoat that was much too small for her. The rain had seeped through, moreover, and the little girl was thoroughly soaked.

"Come in. Come in out of the rain, Iris."

Iris stood on the doorstep and gave her little speech. "I'm not offering to take Dickens for a walk in the rain because I know he doesn't like the rain, but I wonder if you would let me come in for a while, until I can go home?"

"Come in, dear. Come in." Tears rushed to Maggie's eyes and she threw the door wide open and knelt to give the little girl a hug. "You'll need a drying out and then I'll make you some hot chocolate. And we'll give Dickens his dog treats."

Dickens joined them at the mention of treats.

She led Iris to the guest bathroom, where she gave her a fluffy white towel and told her to undress if she wanted and get thoroughly dry and put on the bathrobe hanging on the back of the door. By then the hot chocolate should be ready.

When they were seated at the kitchen table with their hot chocolate and cat-tongue cookies, Maggie said, "Now what's this business of not being able to go home until five o'clock?

That doesn't make a lot of sense, does it. So long as there's somebody home."

"My daddy's home. But he's working."

David came into the kitchen then, still groggy from his nap and surprised to find Iris there. "Iris!" he said. "What are you doing here? Is everything all right?"

"I'm visiting Mrs. Holliss," Iris said. "And Dickens."

"We're visiting," Maggie said, "and we're having hot chocolate and we weren't planning on being interrupted by any grumpy people."

Chastised and no longer groggy, David said, "Well, it's certainly nice to see you, Iris." He noticed then that she was wearing the guest bathrobe. "Are you okay? Or just wet?"

"I was wet but I'm dry now."

"Well, you two have a nice visit. I'm going to go read until it's time to watch *Judge Judy*." He left them to their hot chocolate.

Maggie and Iris sipped their drinks and waited until he had gone. Then Iris said, in a conspiratorial tone, "My daddy watches *Judge Judy*."

"I watch *Judge Judy*. Everybody watches *Judge Judy*. Actually, in this house it's David who watches *Judge Judy*. I just keep him company."

"That's why I can't go home. She's part of his research." Iris sat back and waited.

Maggie looked at Iris and decided this was not an accidental betrayal of her father. The child understood what she was saying.

"He has to be alone," Iris said.

Maggie was caught up in a conflict of emotions. She was first

THE BEGGAR'S PAWN   ❖   85

of all indignant, outraged that this selfish pig of a man would keep his child out in the rain and the cold while he watched an absurd television program. At the same time she was fascinated that Iris recognized not only that her father was guilty of neglect in keeping her out of the house but also that he must be ashamed to be seen watching a program where semiliterate people brought suit against each other over petty injustices and sometimes, though they scarcely seemed to realize it, over monstrous cruelties. Could an eight-year-old be so sophisticated? Maggie did not know where to begin.

"Why does he have to be alone?" Maggie asked. "Couldn't you watch *Judge Judy* with him?"

Iris smiled shyly. "It's his research"—she quoted her father—"'into the vagaries and follies of human nature.'"

Maggie laughed softly and Iris laughed, too. They stopped, and then they laughed again, together.

"Get dressed, Iris," Maggie said, "and we'll go to Macy's and buy you a new raincoat."

"But my father won't approve," Iris said.

"Your father has *Judge Judy*. You'll have a raincoat."

Iris got dressed.

"And a matching hat. And boots."

PURPLE WAS IRIS'S FAVORITE COLOR and she looked lovely, Maggie said, in her purple raincoat and matching hat and boots. She was telling David, firmly, about taking Iris shopping. No criticism, thank you very much.

"I would have preferred the yellow, but when a child wants purple, she should have purple. And she looked adorable in it."

"You aren't afraid you're interfering?" David was treading carefully because he could see that Maggie had made up her mind on this.

"It's for the welfare of the child."

"But she's somebody else's child."

"Who desperately needed a raincoat."

"I understand. I understand. I understand. But will Parker understand?"

"Well, we'll see, won't we!"

David recognized this as one of those moments when you didn't tangle with Maggie.

"She wants me to shut up, Dickens," he said, and Dickens sighed his elderly sigh. He had lately become used to being invoked as intermediary.

THEY DID NOT HAVE to wait long to see how Reginald would react. He sent Maggie a thank-you card expressing Iris's gratitude for her new purple raincoat—and matching hat and boots—and he added his own thanks for such a generous and practical gift. Instead of a signature, he drew an arrow to indicate there was more on the reverse side where he had written, "A special note: It's so embarrassing to be in need of a loan, but we are grateful to have friends who understand. Please forgive me that I once more find myself in a financial bind and humbly request a loan of four hundred dollars." He signed this special note, "Your grateful friend in the Lord, Reg."

Maggie sat down at once and wrote him a check. She put it in an envelope and walked it to the mailbox at the corner of the street. Then she squared her shoulders, took a deep breath, and went to David's study to tell him everything, nearly. She omitted mentioning that on the previous occasion when Reginald borrowed money, the loan was returned short by two hundred dollars.

Later she wondered why she hadn't told him everything. Why keep back this tiny fact? Because it was damning, that's why. Because it was simply too embarrassing to talk about. Because she was a shirk and a mess. She began to get a headache from so much contrary thinking. *It's a sin of omission*, she told herself. *So shoot me.* But with so much to confess, why not confess this as well? She should take it up with Judge Judy. Or Dickens. Or to hell with it.

10.

The Hollisses had seen little of Reginald in the many weeks since the dinner from hell—and not seeing him pleased them greatly. They would not have been pleased, however, to learn that he had become a regular email correspondent with Claire.

> Cara mia Chiara, you'll never believe the latest. I had finished my day's writing and had prepared tea for Helen and Iris, as is my wont, when my enchanting daughter who had left for school in her pale blue raincoat returned to my home wearing a new purple (purple!) raincoat, with hat and boots to match. Gifts from your mother. Bought without ever asking me or even mentioning to me her intention of doing so. I begin to see why you call her Misery. How could she be so insensitive to my feelings as a father and provider? It is undoubtedly this lack of awareness of other people's feelings that, paradoxically, has made you such a sensitive and feeling woman. The source of your art?

Claire gave a great deal of thought to Reginald's email before she wrote back. What was her mother up to? Was she deliberately interfering in the Parkers' family life or was this just another example of her misdirected good intentions? She thought of the Little Sisters of the Poor and that dull Mother Superior's obsession with charity. Maggie was like that, too. It was another form of self-involvement to intrude like this into somebody's life. She wrote back to Reginald.

> I am tempted to say that their self-indulgence is beyond understanding, except that I have understood it almost from the start. Now *you* begin to understand the Hollisses and you will have the key to understanding me. And my art (if that doesn't sound too grandiose).

For a long time now Claire had underestimated the influence her mother had exerted over her life and career. It was natural enough. As her daughter you had no choice: you either became like Maggie Sedgwick or you revolted against her. The Sedgwick name had early on become a shaping force that Claire had acted against. Being rich, being thin, being kind, being beautiful: these were the code words that influenced what you wore, how much you ate, the way you behaved toward other people even when you didn't like them. Being beautiful had been out of the question, however, and realizing that fact was the start of her rebellion against ever becoming a Sedgwick. She would not be a hypocrite. She would be homely and frank about it and honest.

She found herself famous in high school for her frankness and honesty.

She furthered her rejection of the Sedgwick hypocrisy by

attending Columbia, where people valued her frankness and where just being rude was enough to make you popular.

She joined a commune and left it and formed a lesbian union with Willow.

All this she had explained to Reginald in emails of considerable length and detail over the weeks since the dinner party and their lovemaking that followed it. What she had not truly understood until now was the paradoxical nature of her mother's influence, how this lifetime of pursuing honesty by rebelling against her mother had—a wonderful paradox—led her to her true vocation, acting. For this discovery she experienced a sudden rush of gratitude to her mother and even a kind of hearty affection for her. Good old Misery. With all her imperfections, she was something special. How could you not love her?

Claire wrote a follow-up email to Reginald.

Dear Old Reg: You have to forgive my mother who, I am convinced, meant no harm. She, too, is a victim of her upbringing. You ought to have seen Grandma Sedgwick!!! Early influence is very much in my mind as I prepare my performance of Hedda Gabler, a proto-lesbian victimized by society. More about this later. Love, Chiara.

Reginald read her email and began a reply but decided that he would write the required daily lines of his novel before answering her. It didn't matter how many. Even two or three, if they were good enough, would suffice. Like Hemingway, before he became so crass. To be an authentic artist meant you had to work at it every day, weekends and holidays excepted. As he did.

IRIS STOOD ON THE DOORSTEP in her purple raincoat even though it was not raining and had not been raining for the past three days. She was smiling and eager and was not prepared for Maggie's dour expression. Even Dickens seemed unwelcoming.

"Come in, dear, come in. It's lovely to see you, but I'm sorry that we won't be able to have a long visit today."

Iris, with her highly developed social sense, responded at once. "I can come back some other time, if today isn't convenient. Why don't I do that?" and she turned to leave.

Iris had, in fact, visited almost every afternoon this week. Her visits had been the subject of several short, unpleasant exchanges between David and Maggie. David was charmed by the little girl, though to a lesser extent than Maggie, but he still possessed a strict sense of noninterference in the lives of other people. Or so he insisted. Buying the girl clothes had been bad enough—the request for a loan had followed almost immediately—but this new business of Iris stopping by for a visit nearly every day was positively unwise. Maggie was alienating the girl from her family whether or not that was her intention, and there were bound to be repercussions. There were bound to be consequences. And he didn't mean financial ones. He meant there would be trouble with the Parker clan. Misunderstandings. Fights. And, inevitably, accusations. "You're turning our daughter against us. You're giving her false ideas of her own importance." And then he thought of the ultimate accusation. "Because of you she no longer walks in the way of the Lord." Maggie recognized the rightness of his objections but what David did not understand, she said, was the tenderness of the little girl, her loving nature, the way she returned Maggie to those long-gone days when Claire was eight years old and gave her unconditional love. Yes, yes, I know, he agreed, and it's all good. Except that it's dangerous for the child, stuck as she is in that crazy family, and you've got to make her less dependent on you. In this way Maggie and David decided that, unpleasant though it was, they would have to limit Iris's visits to once a week, and anything they might buy for her would have to be agreed upon beforehand. Together.

And so when Iris stood on the doorstep in her purple raincoat and said, "I can come back some other time, if today isn't convenient," Maggie softened and tears came to her eyes and she said, "Come in, sweetheart, and we'll have a lovely hot chocolate and a chat."

Iris came in and Dickens nuzzled her shyly, as if he was uncertain that this was a good time for pats.

They had their hot chocolate and cookies.

"So you see, once a week is best," Maggie said, having successfully delivered her little speech on limiting the frequency of Iris's visits. They were sitting together on the couch, looking out over the back garden and the leaf-filled swimming pool. "It's better for you, really," Maggie said without conviction. "You'll spend more time with your family. Much as we love you, David and I are not your family, are we? No."

"But I wish you were," Iris said, and leaned her head against Maggie's shoulder. "I wish you were my grandma."

"You already have a grandma. Two grandmas, and I'm sure they love you very much."

"I have only one, Grandma Parker," Iris said, burying her face in Maggie's sweater. "And she won't let us visit her. She won't talk to me."

Maggie smoothed the girl's hair and said nothing. What could this mean?

"It's because I'm illegitimate," Iris said.

"Now, now," Maggie said. "I'm sure . . ."

"My mommy and daddy aren't married and so I'm illegitimate."

"But we know they love you very much." Maggie was suddenly filled with indignation. This poor child. Her poor mother. Men were swine, really, they were. Except for David. Even her own two sons were swine, Sedge with a new marriage every few years and Will abandoning his wife and three daughters for a graduate student half his age. And now Reginald, using and abusing poor Helen and depriving Iris of a proper grandma. *She* could be Iris's grandma! She'd be a devoted and loving grandma. She found herself about to say, *All men are swine, Iris, you should learn that while you're young*, but she caught herself in time and said, "All men are different, Iris, and I'm sure your mother and father have excellent reasons for not marrying. And I'm sure your father loves you all the more for it. I'm sure he's a devoted father."

"He wants me to walk in the way of the Lord."

"We should all walk in the way of the Lord," Maggie said. "And we'll start by walking Dickens. Come on."

So she got herself up off the couch and swept Iris up with her in a big, grandmotherly hug and they took a tired but willing Dickens with them to the dog park.

CLAIRE WROTE REGINALD a lengthy email detailing what life was like growing up with the Hollisses. It was, for Claire, a remarkably sympathetic version of what she had regarded as familial torture while she was a child. She had been obliged to attend concerts, the opera, and on one terrible occasion the ballet. All this was in the interest of cultivating Sedgwick tastes, or perhaps they were merely general tastes appropriate to an academic family, but it was awful in any case. The music was fine and the singing, she supposed, was great, but the awful part was the obligation to spend time with all those old people and to be improved in the process. She never felt improved. She felt attacked for not enjoying the higher reaches of culture. These experiences warped her, she knew, but now she recognized that they had kept her from discerning that her life did indeed lie with the arts. She was born to act.

And yet, as Reginald's emails had helped her to realize, her mother had been a formative influence for the good. She had unintentionally helped Claire to become the Claire of today. Maggie had encouraged her passion for seeing things as they are and approved her determination to speak the truth no matter how unpleasant and allowed her to develop her fierce integrity. "She has, without intending it, helped me move toward the light," Claire wrote, and for the moment she felt moved almost to tears.

Reginald wrote back, pleased that he had helped her to new insight regarding her past life and her present devotion to art.

Chiara mia: It pleases me greatly to hear that you have achieved such a benevolent understanding of your early life with your mother and I am prepared to grant you the validity of your conclusions.

I continue, however, to find her interference in our lives to be a remarkable thing. Nonetheless I am trying to see her actions from your point of view, and to that end I have borrowed four hundred dollars from her to take my family to Chantilly for Thanksgiving dinner. You know the restaurant, of course. Très grand. Certainly the grandest here in Palo Alto.

I'm certain your mother would not regard this as an emergency, but that's because, in the minds of the rich, the poor are not supposed to rejoice but merely to survive. Perhaps I can instruct her a little with my own brand of fierce integrity.

Paradoxically yours, Reg

This response delighted and amused Claire, who found it easy to imagine her mother's frustration and her father's stroke-inducing rage when they learned how the latest emergency loan was used. And they would learn about it, she was certain. Ironies this rich could never be kept quiet.

She wrote him back: "No wonder I love you."

How wonderful it was just to watch what would happen, with no ill feeling toward anyone, with just a keen eye out for what could be used in her art.

IT WAS FRIDAY, raining again, and David joined Maggie and Iris for a cozy chat in the living room. He had his cup of tea while they had their hot chocolate. The gas fire burned brightly in the fireplace and the atmosphere was lazy and warm and David placed his feet on the hassock, saying, "I'm going to toast these feet thoroughly, Iris, and I'll never be chilly again. What do you think about that?"

"I think that's nice," Iris said. She was not as comfortable with David as she was with Maggie. After a moment's pause she asked, "Did you have a nice Thanksgiving?"

They both said at once that they had had a very nice Thanksgiving. In fact it had been a tense dinner with their son Sedge, who had driven up from Los Angeles for the day. He had brought with him his new friend, Sophia, who worked in costume design for Columbia Pictures and who would undoubtedly become the next Mrs. Sedge Holliss. Everyone was relieved when it was over.

"And how was your Thanksgiving, Iris?" David asked. "Did you have a turkey?"

"But they're vegetarians," Maggie said. "They don't have turkey." And to Iris she said, "Did your mother make one of her lovely special meals?"

"We had turkey because it was Thanksgiving," Iris said. "My daddy said, 'This is an exception and it's Thanksgiving' and he took us to Chantilly for dinner. It's a restaurant." In the silence that followed, she said, "It's a very nice restaurant."

"Well, good for you," Maggie said. "Did you like the turkey?"

"Chantilly," David said, growing pale at the thought. "Chantilly is a very fine restaurant."

"My daddy said, 'We'll have turkey and a superior white wine.' And he said, 'It's a poor heart that never rejoices.'"

"And your daddy's right," David said. "Your daddy is absolutely right."

11.

Reginald had suspected that Claire was falling in love with him. It was one thing to have a go-for-it, balls-out sexual fling but quite another to allow it to turn into a love affair. He suspected or at least feared this was happening and so he took care to hold her at a little distance. "Very preoccupied with my book," he wrote her. "Significant changes in the making." Having written this, he actually began to see that changes were necessary and good. And indeed significant.

As he had suggested at their dinner party and as he had explained to Claire in the greatest detail the day following, his novel was a study in big ideas—the metaphysics of personality—but it was much more than that. It was a psychological thriller and a neo-epistemological detective story.

"And what is that?" Claire asked.

"My novel."

"No. What is a neo-epistemological detective story?"

"Neo-epistemological merely means it's a whydunit. I investigate not only the nature of the crime but the nature of the criminal as well. Whodunit, plus why. You have to sense it before you can understand it. You can't get bogged down in terminology," he said. "And by the end of the book I'll demonstrate that we can never know the nature of character and personality in their totality."

"Don't we know that already?"

"See, it all becomes one vast circle."

"A vicious circle," Claire said.

"These are some of the ideas I explore. The story itself is about a man who is writing a novel about a man who is writing a novel about a nineteenth-century novelist who may or may not have been the father of Jack the Ripper's final victim. So the story is one vast circle as well. I explore the fifth dimension."

"Fascinating," Claire said. "Who's the novelist?"

"Dickens, but my character is gonna be more philosophical than Dickens. Sort of a combination of Dickens and Heidegger. Heidegger said, 'What matters most is to listen to what is not being said.' So that's my title: *What Is Not Being Said*."

"Fascinating. Really."

"But I'm thinking of changing Dickens to Gissing." He had laughed lightly, wickedly.

Claire laughed with him. "Poop will have a stroke," she said. She was vastly entertained. She quite liked this change from Dickens to Gissing. She quite liked Reg himself, though he was nothing to crow about in bed, conserving his creativity and inspiration for his work, no doubt. In bed he remained methodical, uninspired.

REGINALD'S INTENTIONS to discourage her from falling in love with him were completely lost on Claire. "How exciting," she wrote about his plans for the novel, "I want to know all about it. Meanwhile let me catch you up on my discoveries about Hedda Gabler." And here she proceeded to expound at prodigious length on the similarities between Hedda's family problems and her own. "Hedda has no mother; mine was a mess. Hedda's father was a general who left her nothing but his name and his dueling pistols. Mine was the same, practically, except he's an academic. Our backgrounds really are almost identical, right down to Hedda's great, unexplained feeling of inadequacy. The dueling pistols (Penis! Penis!) are the instruments of her creativity: she persuades her lover to use one of them to commit suicide and she kills herself with the other. I realize now that it's been my father all along who has blighted my life, not my mother. He's the one who has made me feel inadequate: not sufficiently a woman, too much a man. By the end of the play what's left for Hedda except enlightenment or suicide? As I play her, she has no choice. As for me, I choose enlightenment."

She added in a separate paragraph: "See how useful our time in bed has been?" And she signed off, "Hugs and kisses, Chiara tua."

HUGS AND KISSES INDEED. Well, perhaps she meant this to be a merely conventional sign-off but it made him uncomfortable all the same. He clicked the Chiara icon to make sure it could not be accessed, double-checked it, and logged out. Time to make tea for Helen.

"My one true love," he sometimes said to her, and he meant it insofar as love was useful. There had been other sexual relationships before Claire, and Helen knew about them in that way that wives know and do not know. That is, she was sure he was having sex with somebody else, she knew when the affair started and when it was over, but she was quite happily spared the details. Much better not to know names and places, much better not to have a mental picture of the rival who was of merely sexual interest. That interest would pass, sometimes with bitterness but most often with merely the awareness that it was over, and goodbye, goodbye to another anonymous woman who had shared Reginald's bed but not his heart or his mind.

Helen came through the door, tired and with her hair uncombed and her lipstick faded, and Reginald greeted her, "Helen, my one true love." How good she was. How safe she was. How passionately she believed in him.

HELEN HAD NO INTEREST in Reginald's emails and no temptation to spy on him. Iris, however, was possessed of a limitless curiosity and not only curiosity but an ability to use computers with a beginner's expertise. She was rarely alone in the house, but when she was, she used her time to advantage. Thus Iris was aware of the range and depth of the relationship between Reginald and Claire long before her mother had begun to suspect anything. But with her natural intelligence and her eagerness to protect her mother, Iris said nothing. She just made a point of checking "Chiara" as often as possible and turning these things over in her heart, knowing betrayal was part of her father's legacy, just like Hedda Gabler's father, whoever he was.

"HAVE YOU READ CLAIRE'S EMAIL?" Maggie asked.

David and Maggie shared an email address so that whatever was sent to one of them was accessed by both.

"I'm wary of her emails these days," David said. "She's getting crisper and crisper."

"Meaning?"

"More brittle, more biting. There's always a little arrow to the heart in everything she writes. She thinks she's found ultimate truth in Hedda Gabler. That bodes ill, if you ask me."

"Actually, she thanks you for helping her understand Hedda Gabler. She has just now recognized what a big influence you were on her, she says. I thought I was the big influence. At least I always got the blame."

"She was never a happy girl."

"'The still point of the turning world.'"

"Well, I'm glad to be the newest big influence, but I can't help feeling it's going to turn out bad."

"Badly."

"Pedant."

"Give us a kiss."

They shared a perfunctory, serviceable kiss.

"Those dueling pistols are going to come into this eventually."

"Not really. This is life, not literature."

———

CLAIRE'S PREPARATION FOR playing Hedda was thorough and, from the start, dissatisfying. She had envisioned performing before an enraptured New York audience but scaled back her expectations as her private rehearsals went on and on and her acting coach, the former Broadway actress, grew increasingly critical. And unfriendly. "More feeling, more desperation," her coach said. "This is a beautiful woman of the nineteenth century, not a truck driver of the twentieth. She is hopelessly repressed and she knows it, but she can't really connect with a man sexually. She is afraid of men and she is sexually attracted to them and she has nowhere to turn. She is boring herself to death. She says so herself. She could be a great pagan if only she could let herself go."

"I am a great pagan. I can let myself go."

"Acting is not the same as life. Acting has to be more real than life."

This was true but Claire resented being told what she already knew.

"My father was like Hedda's father. He never really saw me. He left me only his pistols."

"What are you talking about? You told me your father is a professor of English literature. He's alive in California. How is he leaving you dueling pistols?"

"Metaphorically. He's left me his penis."

"Let's get back to Hedda Gabler. Hedda has no penis. That's the issue."

Rehearsals grew more disappointing and the acting coach more dissatisfied. Claire was depressed. It did not help that during rehearsals all the other characters were played by that old has-been with the script in her hand, the bitch. She kept telling Claire to dig deeper, dig deeper, but Claire had already dug down past her domineering mother to the quick soil of her neglectful, selfish, inadequate father. Asked to identify some mitigating virtue in the foul mix of his character, Claire came up with evidence that he was insecure. He had only written two books in his entire career . . . because he was afraid. Afraid to fail. Perhaps even afraid to succeed. As rehearsals progressed, she became more interested in his failure as an academic, as a man, as a father. He was inadequate and insecure. Look at the wreckage he had made of his sons' lives. The family was a disaster. Their only genuine affection was for a dog called Dickens.

She wrote about these discoveries to Reginald and he wrote back asking for more, and more.

He liked getting to know her in this way, he said, he liked learning all about the Hollisses.

IRIS READ THE EMAILS between Claire and her father and pondered whether or not she should tell her mother. Her father, she knew, was a genius, and she knew, too, that geniuses did not have to observe the rules. Her mother had explained this often enough. Her father was special. He was a philosophical novelist and so he didn't go out to work like other men. He worked at home. He worked all the time. Even when he watched *Judge*

Judy, he was working. But until now Iris had not known about other women in his life.

Uncertain how to respond to this new information about her father, she began slowly to withdraw from her mother and to lavish more affection on him. It was compensation for not loving him anymore.

Iris wondered, should she talk to Mrs. Holliss about this?

IN THE INTEREST of accumulating more material for his novel Reginald had put aside his worries that Claire was hell-bent on a love affair. He could always handle that later. What mattered now was collecting and sorting all this good, *Judge Judy*-ish information on the Hollisses' family picnic. He wrote to Claire explaining that he liked knowing that theirs was an intellectual and artistic friendship and not just something patched together following an afternoon's roll in the hay. Tell me more, he said, tell me more.

CLAIRE'S PERFORMANCE as Hedda took place in Baltimore's New Repertory Theatre on a Sunday afternoon. The stage was set for the current production of *You Can't Take It with You*, not an ideal background for the mental anguish of Hedda Gabler, and the audience consisted of Willow, the backstage crew, and the members of the advisory board of the repertory company. The issue, as put to them by Willow, was whether or not they should stage a full-scale production of this difficult play. In fact, the issue had been all but decided. The advisory board had been thrilled with Claire's performance as Grandma in *The American Dream*, but in the many months since that production they had discovered that Claire was Grandma on- and offstage, all the time, in every situation. She was tart talking, smart-alecky, pleased with herself. She was physically awkward and unappealing. She made a great snarky Grandma but how could this translate into the subtle complexities of Hedda Gabler? Nonetheless, to please Willow, who was so hardworking and such a good sort, they had decided to let Claire audition for the role by doing a solo performance of Hedda, with Willow reading all the other parts from the side of the stage.

The performance, they concluded, was a disaster.

In fact, the performance might have been a success had it been heard and not seen. Claire had managed to tap into some of the unidentified desperations of her own life and brought them to bear on the character of Hedda. Her strident voice had been softened and smoothed out by her vocal coach, and Claire had managed to give an ironic and sometimes even funny twist to Hedda's repartee with her husband and his aunt and her would-be lover. Her sense of Hedda as a desperate woman had been deepened by all her digging into her own past and to those discoveries she had added her ruminations on Reginald's wife, Helen, and her odd position as acolyte to her husband's genius. In the end she had a sense of who Hedda was and what made her a doomed woman.

In her own mind, Claire's performance was both true and good, and what more could you ask? What she failed to perceive was that physically she was not prepared for the stage at all. She had no sense of stage space and how to occupy it. She had no natural grace. She moved with difficulty. She was short and square, she acknowledged that. She was unaware, however, that she was in herself awkward, that her gestures failed to come naturally, that she clutched at the furniture as if she could negotiate the stage only by lurching from chair to chair. And when it came time to kill herself, she grasped the pistol as if she were terrified it might go off.

And so, after all her work, it came as a great shock that nobody laughed where she had anticipated laughter, nobody cringed when she physically attacked her rival, Thea, snatching at her hair and then smothering her in an embrace, and nobody gasped in horror as she blew out her brains.

Worse still was the polite applause that followed her death.

And worst of all was the gentle way the advisory board explained the decision not to stage *Hedda Gabler*, at least not now, at least not with Claire playing Hedda.

She was inconsolable, she wrote Reginald, she wanted to kill herself. She had achieved personal truth in performance and nobody cared. It was enough to turn her against acting for good. But she would keep on. She had learned that much from playing Hedda: good old Claire would never kill herself.

REGINALD WAS DELIGHTED with Claire's emails. They struck just the right balance between friendship and love. They were trusting, detailed, and confessional. They indicated that she was discovering what he had always known: that the life of the artist is one of unremitting pain and effort, that you can't expect to be loved and admired in this world, that the constant temptation to kill yourself must be—in most cases—resisted. Better to kill someone else. And thus they both placed blame where it belonged, on her father.

Reginald wrote her a quick email and sent it on at once. Be brave, he said, and remember that only art is eternal. He had decided to put off telling her details of the proposed changes in his novel.

PART THREE

❖ ❖ ❖

12.

That was the year—2010—when the East Coast toasted in an untimely winter heat and the West Coast had its coldest summer ever. It was the year of the greatest oil disaster . . . so far. But more remarkable still, that was the year when anger, professionalized and politicized, turned into hate. There were threats to burn the Koran, there were pickets and rallies against building a Muslim cultural center near ground zero, there was conviction in the radical American heart that anger could make all things right, for anger was mighty and it was good. And it begins at home.

Reginald's family home was in Hillsborough, but he did not go there anymore. Everybody in Hillsborough—servants and laborers excepted—had money somewhere in their past. Their great houses clung to the side of hills where views were most expansive and the more visible signs of wealth were concealed behind a faux rustic exterior. This was old wealth, modest about public exposure. It was also wealth that in many cases, and in Reginald's particularly, had been greatly depleted over time. What was left to the Parkers was barely enough to cover taxes and upkeep, pay a cook and a daily cleaner, and stable the two family horses now enjoying old age. But not enough for what they regarded as luxuries.

Reginald's grandmother and his mother were now the sole occupants of the house and together they ran the cook half-crazy with their constant quarrels and their contradictory orders. Life would have been impossible if not for the Scottish cleaning woman who showed up each morning eager and ready to administer her bracing tonic.

"I see you're picking up after yourself these days," she said to the grandmother. "It's a good habit to get into. I won't work for careless people." And to the daughter she said, "Easy on the sherry, missy. You'll lose your looks."

Her unrelenting belligerence kept her employers in their place and brought a welcome peace to the household. She slammed through her cleaning tasks at double time and later, over coffee, she cheered on the harried cook with tales of other dysfunctional families she had brought to heel. "You have to know how to handle the quality, and the Parkers are no exception. They just need reminding now and then." The grandmother, cowed and at the mercy of the cleaning woman, paid her well.

They lived in a state of armed neutrality, with Reginald as the territory they fought over. The grandmother still had some personal money left and frequently mailed Reginald small checks. Despite his repeated failures, she held out hope for his familial success.

His mother, who continued to go by her Junior League name of Boo, wore out her days steeped in Spanish sherry and dreamed of another life. A life without Reginald. She blamed him for being born illegitimate, since his handsome father would never have decamped and married someone else if she hadn't been pregnant. She blamed him for ruining her looks, since his birth caused her to put on weight, and still more weight. She blamed him for being carefree and careless. But what turned her against him for good was his young cruelty. At age five he set their cat on fire and a year later he tried to burn down the garage. The fire was extinguished before it did much damage but later that summer, already advanced in crime, he tried to drown his best friend. Boo had no proof of the attempted drowning except the testimony of appalled club members—you could never trust club members—but she was sure he was guilty and promised herself she was done with him. She kept her promise as each new year brought further conviction that she was right.

Boo indeed! She found consolation in her sherry and in her occasional performance as docent at the local museum. For physical consolation she enjoyed brief sexual encounters with the pool cleaner, the groundsman, and, when she was weak and he was willing, with the odd delivery man of any age or color. Most of her time she spent watching soap operas and waiting for her mother to die . . . with the reasonable expectation that the family money and property would come to her. In this she was mistaken, however, since on turning eighty her mother revised her will so that the property was left to the Hillsborough Green Society and the bulk of the money went to the rescue of neglected animals. At the urging of her lawyer she left a token hundred thousand to keep Boo in sherry and a niggardly one thousand to the Scots cleaning woman. She had not yet decided about leaving anything to her grandson.

The grandmother's disappointment in Reginald began when as a freshman at St. Paul's he was expelled for smoking pot. The first offense was easily forgiven and so were the third and fourth, but when in his junior year he began dealing drugs, his grandmother gave him an ultimatum: stop or be cut off financially. He pretended to stop and by his senior year the pretense had been so well practiced that it became a reality . . . and he was further helped by his discovery that he had a talent for writing. He sailed through senior year, graduated with honors, and went off to Duke to become a responsible member of the Parker family. Grandmother sent monthly checks to remind him of those responsibilities.

At first everything went well. He had drinking buddies and smoking buddies, all from good families like his own, and, with his funny hair and tiny eyes, he was inexplicably popular with the girls. In his second semester he discovered Joyce's *Ulysses* and resolved to spend the rest of his life becoming the new Joyce and writing *Ulysses, Part Two*. But Duke was not interested in ambitious new fiction. Instead they made him write boring essays on set topics that elicited annoying comments like "Clarity, lack of" and "Misused language" and "Your point here?" Reginald dropped out of Duke and went home. But you can't go home again, he discovered. Both his mother and grandmother complained about the smell of pot all through the house, the cleaning woman refused to go near his room, and Reginald decided to clear out. He rented a studio apartment in the Haight district of San Francisco, where he could smoke in peace while he practiced his exacting art. Money was a problem of course but on the day he was born his errant father had set up a trust for him so that when Reginald turned twenty-five he could collect a hundred dollars a week. His father then disappeared into a succession of bad marriages and was lost finally to alimony and alcohol. But he had done his bit and Reginald would have been grateful if only the trust had been larger and available immediately. Still, it was something to look forward to. In the meanwhile he panhandled and he clerked from time to time at Walgreens and became an expert at shoplifting. Eventually he turned twenty-five and got his money.

His trust fund made life a bit easier. And so did the drugs. In time, however, the drugs got to be too much for him—cocaine regularly and the odd touch of heroin—and he began to give way to violent rages. These culminated one night in a complete black-out that followed a bloody fight with his sixteen-year-old drug dealer. There was a knife involved—neither of them was willing to claim it—and Reginald found himself accused of assault with intent to do bodily harm. He spent a week in jail before his grandmother's lawyer got the charges reduced to a misdemeanor and, chastened at last, Reginald dragged himself off to a Buddhist monastery where he dried out and thought about his life and his talent. For a dizzy moment he considered becoming a Buddhist monk, but when he returned to his senses he recognized that he was—by birth and disposition—a novelist in the great Western tradition and he just couldn't hack all that Eastern mysticism. Instead he began freeloading at Glide Memorial Church, where he picked up the Christian notion of your brother's keeper—very serviceable for panhandling—and he began to talk about the Lord's way and walking with Jesus. It was non-sense, but it appealed to the do-gooders who had access to cash and who enjoyed helping the needy. Reginald enjoyed the Lord's way. At times all this born-again business made good sense. He would have enjoyed sitting back and relaxing into belief if he didn't have to worry about getting a job and if believing weren't so lonely. What he needed was to love someone, he was convinced, or to have someone love him . . . the way a mother and father would love him. Or better still, the right girl. All the girls he met were hookers or druggies or losers of one kind or another, so what was he supposed to do? Write? He was desperate.

He decided to get serious about his career. He took an evening course in fiction writing at San Francisco State and resolved to write at least one page a day. He stayed off drugs . . . with only a little marijuana on the weekend. He was ready for intense work. But when he returned to Joyce and *Ulysses* and his great unwritten novel, he discovered he had outgrown his earlier ambitions. They sounded dull and conventional now. Never mind.

He was off drugs and feeling good. In fact he was feeling lucky.

He would write a new kind of novel, something that had never been done before, a novel in which time and eternity mate, a kind of fifth-dimension novel—black holes included—where the great issues of philosophy could be explored. He was ready for a new life. He looked for an apartment close to Stanford so that those keen practitioners of physics and philosophy would be at hand when he needed them. His luck held and he found a guest cottage owned by Professor Loring and his wife. His grandmother, relieved that he was off drugs and still sane, agreed to pay the rent.

Over the next years there was not a lot of mingling with great minds but Reginald did meet Helen, a barista at the nearby Starbucks, and so great was her love for him and so overwhelming her belief in his genius that eventually he capitulated and let her move into his guest cottage. Maybe this is what came of walking in the way of the Lord. He thought he might give it a try. Helen's adoration persisted and he began to imagine new possibilities for his own life. It was almost like falling in love. "I love you. I adore you," she said, and he pressed her closer to him and whispered, "I know, I know." When she got pregnant he saw in this a kind of guarantee that she was right for him. "I love you," he told her, and he was astonished to find that he meant it. The idea of marriage crossed his mind but he put it aside as he had his temptation to be a Buddhist monk. It was enough that they were together and she believed he could—he would—become a great writer. And he would be a father as well. He took some coke to celebrate . . . and this would be the last time.

The illegitimate Iris proved the final straw for Reginald's mother and she cut him off altogether. Again. Reginald shrugged. He had a family at last, a wife and daughter who loved him and depended on him. He didn't need Boo. He still had his trust fund—a weekly hundred wasn't nothing—and good old Grandma kept on paying the rent, chiefly to spite her outraged daughter. So he would be able to get on with his novel, which was the important thing.

At the time he met Maggie and David he had still not finished the novel. And not long after that meeting he gave up on it altogether. He began a new one, more elegant, more streamlined,

13

Reginald was convinced that David, despite his height and weight and the authority in his voice, was in fact the weaker of the two Hollisses. From all those years in the classroom David had become deft at fending off irrelevant or annoying questions and he could be plain rude as well, but Reginald was pretty sure he could handle him. A direct request to Maggie might bring on a direct refusal, but David would be a pushover. He'd be worried what people would think of him and so he'd temporize and then give in.

He found them at the dog park. They were sitting together, young lovers, on a bench.

"What's up?" David said, a formality only.

"Meditating my book," Reginald said. "And my problems."

David showed elaborate interest in a Yorkie that was trying to involve Dickens in play. Dickens just wanted to be left alone.

"Oh, your book. The metaphysical mystery," Maggie said. "*Petit à petit.*"

"Pardon?"

"Little by little. Rome wasn't built in a day. It takes time to write a book."

"You can say that again."

"No, I think saying it was a mistake the first time around."
So that ended that.

"Actually, I have a question for David. A request, actually."

David's face flushed red for a moment and then it went white.
He continued to study the Yorkie.

"Yes, I wonder if you would loan me three hundred dollars?"
He waited in silence, resisting the temptation to offer a reason
for the request or a promise of repayment, letting the silence do
its work. He watched David's face closely and could see him
processing questions and objections and reasons to say no.

Reginald waited.

Maggie, grateful that this was David's problem, said nothing.

David was thinking of all the checks he'd written for his three
kids and their hopeless problems. He made up his mind quickly.

"Yes," David said. "If you come back to the house with us, I'll
write you a check."

THEY GAVE DICKENS his dog treats and settled into the breakfast nook with a cup of coffee. David had written the check and
Reginald had left the house and now they were unwinding. Neither of them wanted to mention the loan.

"Poor Iris," Maggie said.

"Poor *us*," David said. "How did we get into this mess in the
first place?"

"It was my fault. He saved Dickens's life and I loaned him
two hundred dollars."

"Right. That first loan."

She couldn't let this go unchallenged. "And you gave him a picnic basket of champagne and stuff. Piper Heidsieck."

"Charles Heidsieck."

"And then we went to dinner at his place. Dear God, that dinner!"

They thought about the dinner for a while.

"Why did you loan him another three hundred? I thought we agreed that this last one would be the last one?"

"He caught me off guard. I never expected a frontal attack. Would you have refused him?"

"I'd have just given it to him with no loan agreement at all, just for the sake of Iris."

"Well next time that's what I'll do. I'll say, 'Here's the money. It's not a loan. You can pay us back . . . if that's possible . . . or you can just keep the money, all the money, as a gift. But this is the final . . . thing.'"

"'Thing'?"

"Payment. Handout. Payoff. Bribe. What should I call it?"

"The final money."

"That's what I'll say. You can pay us back if you choose to or you can just regard it as a gift, but whatever you decide, this is the absolutely final money."

"The final money. And if he asks me, I'll tell him he has to ask you. So that we're both in agreement."

"Is that settled?"

"It's settled," Maggie said and finished her coffee.

"So we've solved that problem, Dickens."

Dickens thumped his tail on the floor in response.

REGINALD WROTE CLAIRE a lengthy email about the changes in his novel. He began diplomatically by acknowledging the justice of everything she had written about her father: his inadequacy, his self-interest, his insecurity.

"It's all true," Reginald wrote. "I saw them in the park this morning, sitting on a bench like two lovebirds, and they looked so annoying that I asked him for three hundred dollars to get high." He pondered this for a moment and decided that borrowing money for a Thanksgiving dinner at Chantilly might amuse her, but borrowing three hundred for pot and just a little hit of coke might not. So he deleted the whole email and started again.

> Chiara mia: Changes in my novel. I have opted for simplicity and have dropped the novelist who is writing about a novelist, etc. etc. who may have been the father of Jack the Ripper's final victim. I've decided to take out several layers—no fifth dimension, no Jack the Ripper—and write about a biographer instead, a man like your father who is very distinguished but in his old age has undertaken a biography of Stephen Crane.

Actually, Reginald had written Gissing rather than Crane, but he realized suddenly that there was rich material he could borrow from David's second biography and he had immediately changed Gissing to Crane. It occurred to him then that he was in a sense borrowing David's career as the subject of his novel, and why not? David was seventy-something and had no further need of it anyhow. Indeed, why not borrow his whole life? And if you're borrowing his life, why not borrow his family? The entire horror show. His mind reeled for a moment and his head fell forward as if he had been assaulted from behind. His sight went all fuzzy. Here at last was inspiration, an idea so powerful it made his head spin. He found himself erect and covered with sweat. So this was the real thing. He was a writer at last.

He deleted the entire email and started fresh.

Cara mia: Vast changes in my novel. I think I told you already that I've given up the idea of a novel about a novelist, etc. etc. and replaced it with a biographer writing a biography, etc. etc. but just today I decided on a much more radical change. I ran into your father and mother in the park and, while chatting with them, a whole new novel came to me: a study of contemporary life as seen through the lives of a dysfunctional family—my own, of course, not yours. This means jettisoning the fifth dimension and writing in a much more traditional form. I worry that I am giving in to the demands of the market but my muse tells me this is the story I must write.

He was still erect and gave some thought to masturbation but decided instead to wait until Helen got home from Walmart and let her discover yet again what a real writer was capable of.

14

The serious winter rains fell in January and the lion-colored hills around Palo Alto turned green overnight. The weather was cold for Northern California and it was dark by five o'clock and the combination of cold and dark proved enough for David Holliss. He retired from the university and from the English department. He had plenty to do. Research on Gissing promised to take him into oldest old age and there were books to read that he had always meant to get to someday and there was some interesting Home Box Office stuff to watch on television. And Netflix, of course. So the full, rich life of the intellect could continue without the burden of reading one more term paper or directing another PhD dissertation. What he disliked most of all was telling students their work was fine except for this and this and this and so you'd better just start over. And to be honest, David told Maggie, I was always slightly over my head in the English department and it's a relief not to feel I have to live up to their standards. I'm at heart a vulgarian, and *Judge Judy*, he said, is just my speed.

The winter rains trickled away in early April, and soon the hills turned ocher and amber and pale yellow, and David and right side of his head. He had been dreaming he was a prisoner at Guantanamo Bay and they were subjecting him to enhanced interrogation by hammering a nail, slowly, with small taps, into the side of his head. It hurt so much that he sat up in bed, rigid with pain. *A stroke*, he said to himself, and he was right. He pushed himself out of bed and took a step in the direction of the bathroom and felt his hand slide down the wall until he was sitting cross-legged on the floor. He listened for a moment but there was no movement from Maggie. He tried to call her but succeeded only in making a small croaking sound. Maggie stirred in her bed and continued to sleep. Dickens, who slept across the doorway, came to inquire what was going on. It was two or two thirty in the morning—David could barely make out the clock—so he was on his own. Stroke or not, however, he could still think straight. You couldn't call a doctor at this hour. And, since it was Sunday night, there was no point in going to the emergency room, where the janitors and their assistants would be taking blood and performing operations. The thing was to keep on thinking clearly. The thing was to get through this without making a fuss. The thing was . . . He tried to stand by pushing against the nightstand and working his way up the wall with his right hand as a kind of grappling hook and in a minute or two he had done it. He was standing. His left arm still had feeling in it though his left leg was useless. It was made of rubber and gave way under the least pressure. He took a deep breath and determined to go on. Leaning against the wall and pushing himself along with his right arm, he managed to stagger down the corridor to his study. It all looked different in the semi-dark, but he found his desk chair and collapsed into it and rested. He was rather proud of himself. He was surviving.

"Good boy," he tried to say to Dickens, who curled up at his feet.

A blood clot, he decided, as bad as the first time, and maybe worse. So long as it doesn't rupture. So long as the blood can find its way around the clot. What he had to do was keep his brain functioning and somehow get through the night.

He picked up his worn copy of *New Grub Street*. Surely Gissing would help preserve whatever brainpower he still had. He began to read the introduction but the words failed to make any sense. He turned ahead to the familiar opening pages and after a while he began to follow Gissing's story about the cruelty and barbarism of the publishing industry. He forced himself to read on and on and he was still reading in the morning when Maggie came down the corridor and asked, rhetorically, "What are you doing? Have you lost your mind?"

His speech was thick and muddied but he was able to mumble, "It well may be," and she realized at once what had happened.

THE RECEPTIONIST AT THE EMERGENCY room was unimpressed. She had seen strokes before and the patients were usually delivered flat on their backs by ambulance. This one was standing at her desk and speaking, more or less, though it was true that he had propped himself up with his right arm. He seemed altogether too cheery for a stroke victim. She assigned him to Dr. Burke, who was the newest intern. He was cute and upbeat and could use the experience, she figured. Dr. Burke, who looked fourteen, was succeeded by several other interns who were also fourteen, and finally David was examined by an elderly doctor of twenty-six who confirmed that indeed he had had some kind of stroke. How bad it was and whether or not it had yet run its course remained a mystery. He would need an MRI and an MRA and a CAT scan before they could make a determination. Meanwhile he should think about his choices for a living will. If it came to the final crunch, did he want to be resuscitated or not? Did he want to refuse all extraordinary survival measures? For instance, some patients wanted to exclude intubation. How did he feel about a tube down his throat?

All this death-or-no-death business came as a surprise to him, and the exhilaration he had felt in realizing he was still alive now took a downturn and he was gripped by a sudden panic. What about Maggie? What about Dickens? What about that goddam Gissing project? His high spirits vanished and he found himself merely embarrassed.

"Choices, choices," he said. "Can't we wait until we see the results of the MRI and the other alphabets?"

The answer was no. After a brief exchange with Maggie, he decided on no extraordinary means of survival, and intubation— yes—providing the breathing tube could be removed if he turned into a vegetable. Maggie would have to make the decision to pull the plug.

They put him in a room with another stroke victim, this one

unable to move or to speak, except to shout "Jesus!" at unexpected moments, and they left him there until they scheduled his brain tests. By that time he had resigned himself to whatever might happen, convinced that even with this third stroke he would be lucky: he'd stroll out of here into a brave new world of low cholesterol and healthy morning walks with Maggie and Dickens.

CLAIRE HAD LONG SINCE given up her hope of playing Hedda Gabler and, having put aside the role, she also put aside her resentment of David, his failures as a father, a husband, a professor of the humanities. "Humanities, ha!" she had written Reginald in those old days, sublimated now and processed in her mind as part of her rich past history of loves and betrayals. She would have been surprised to learn that Reginald had put aside none of these things. They were still fresh in his mind and in his notes and he planned to make excellent use of them.

"Humanities, ha!" she had written, but that was months earlier and long forgotten, and so when Maggie phoned her with the news that David had had another stroke, and this one was the real thing, Claire's first rush of feeling was compassion for her mother, who had to face this all by herself, and then a kind of sadness that so big and energetic a man as David should be brought so low. She saw her father propped up in a wheelchair, head tipped to the side, mouth twisted in an effort to make himself understood. And drooling just a little.

"I'll come home right away," she said.

"I'm calling the others," Maggie said. "It isn't clear yet how bad he is. He hasn't had his MRI or his MRA or his CAT scan. But I wanted you to know, just in case."

So it might be a false alarm. Claire experienced a moment of disappointment, as if she had used up all this sympathy unnecessarily.

"Well," she said. "Shall I come home or not? We're rehearsing a repeat performance of *You Can't Take It with You*, so it's not what you'd call totally convenient for me to come, but I could. I can." She waited for a response, but there was none. "The lighting is all done, really." She waited some more. "Mother?" she said. She realized then that her mother was crying and could not speak. "I'll come home. Poor Mama. Poor Misery. I'll be there tomorrow."

"Only if you can," Maggie said, concealing her momentary anger at Claire's lack of concern for her father. "Only if it's not too much trouble."

MAGGIE CALLED SEDGE and left a message on his home phone. He got back to her late that evening.

"Is this the real thing or is it a TIA?"

"The doctor says it's the real thing. It's his third."

Sedge had rushed up to Palo Alto for the first two strokes only to discover there was nothing he needed to do and nothing he could do. It was just a matter of waiting for the old guy to recover. After the first stroke David had limped a little and then, in a while, he was fine. No residual effects beyond a left hand that sometimes went weak. There was that and a tendency to fall over when he stood up too quickly. Sedge had hung around wasting time. After David's second stroke there had been no ill effects at all.

"The third might be the lucky one." Sedge said this before he thought of what that might mean. He quickly added, "I mean it might be a stroke with no side effects at all."

"I thought you should know," Maggie said. She'd be damned if she was going to ask him to come home.

"I'll come home right away. Do you need anything?"

"Just my husband," she said, angry at the question itself.

"You can count on me."

"I know that," she said, without a trace of sarcasm.

SHE PHONED WILL in Essex. She couldn't recall the time difference—actually, she could but decided she didn't care—and she reached him at three in the morning while he was still in bed with Cloris, the graduate student and wife-to-be.

"I'll call him for you," Cloris said, as if at this hour he was down the corridor in his study.

After a decorous pause, Will said, "Mother? I hope nothing's wrong."

"It's your father," Maggie said. "He's had a small stroke. Nothing too disastrous so far, but the doctors are keeping watch." She was not sure she could handle the return home of Claire and Sedge and Will, all at the same time. "No need to pack a bag yet. I just thought you should know it's happened."

Will at once fell into his Perfect Son mode: "I'll check with British Air in the morning and I should be able to get an emergency flight tomorrow or at the latest the next day. I'll be there, Mother."

"There's no need for alarm, Will," she said. "I just thought you should know . . . in case."

"Cloris will want to come as well. Don't worry about meeting my plane. We'll take a limo from the airport."

"Your father will pull through this, Will. There's no need . . ."

"Lots of love, Mother. See you soon."

All of them home, plus Cloris, the graduate student homewrecker. She couldn't stand even the idea of it.

MAGGIE DID NOT TELL the neighbors about David's stroke that first day. It was too private and too awful to share so she carried on as if nothing had happened. Nonetheless Dickens sensed that something had happened, and the neighbors, being for the most part academics, knew at once that something had happened. Not anything so interesting and final as death, but something disastrous that deserved their consideration and comment. There were no inquiring phone calls and certainly no pop-in visits, just a heightened awareness of what was or was not going on down the street in the Hollisses' house. Nobody wanted to see David dead or even crippled, but there was a certain quiet satisfaction in someone's brush with death that was not—thank God—your own.

DAVID'S MRI AND MRA and CAT scan proved positive for a stroke.

"A large blood clot has settled exactly here in the right side of your head," the doctor said. He looked like a taller, thinner version of Robert Redford—blond hair and all—and patients were always relieved to be in the hands of this eminent neurologist. He was handsome and brilliant; it was almost as if his brilliance were a function of his good looks, and thus the families of the stricken were always unsure whether they were grateful or merely in love. "Exactly here," the doctor said, and with his index finger he touched the very spot where in David's dream they had driven the nail into his skull. "The clot's still there, you can see it on the screen, but the blood has found a path around it and, despite the damage already done, if the blood sticks to that path, you're well away. Give it a week or so."

"'Well away'?" David said.

"Good to go," the handsome doctor said and let his blond hair fall forward on his brow. "All set to live again. Ready for the races."

He shook hands all around. He was the head of the department of neurology and had many more people to see and so he left them, grateful as they were, and went ahead on his glamorous way.

David had been lucky for the third time. Was there no end to his good fortune?

THE HANDSOME DOCTOR SHOWED him images of his brain. "Do you see those white spots? Those are dead matter. They show up in all the slides. They indicate where neurotransmitters have failed. No surprise. This is, after all, your third stroke—the first two were just blips on the screen—but you're well into your seventies. What are you, seventy-four, seventy-five? You've earned your dead spots."

"But my speech isn't affected. Or my thinking. Has my thinking been affected?"

"Only you would know. Best to look on the bright side. We'll give you blood thinners and you'll be good to go. Just be careful not to fall or hit your head." He patted David on the shoulder. "Good man," he said, already on his way, "good news, good news."

It was decided, despite the good news, to keep David in the hospital until the likelihood of another stroke had passed. A few days, perhaps a week.

Hearing this, David lost some of his optimism. And as they suggested he might, he became unsteady on his feet, he limped a little, and he kept waiting for that bloody tsunami to slosh through his brain. So that when Claire flew in from Baltimore to give consolation to her mother and a decent burial to her father, she found a rather sulky, depressed old man who looked as if he should be dying but showed no signs of doing so.

laire was the first to arrive. Maggie met her at the airport and very nearly failed to recognize her. From her Broadway coach Claire had learned something about the art of makeup, and in the debacle over staging *Hedda Gabler* she had lost fifteen pounds, not a great deal in itself but for someone short and square the loss proved transformative. Her hair was cut fashionably short and streaked in auburn, lending a kind of feathery halo to her face. This was a new Claire and Maggie was for the moment struck silent.

"Mother!" Claire said. "Mommy!" she said. "Poor Misery! Tell me he's still alive."

Maggie took Claire in her arms and cried softly. She was still speechless at how good Claire looked.

"Is he? Is he still alive?"

"You look so wonderful," Maggie said. "Just wonderful. Your father won't recognize you."

"I'm not sure how you mean that."

"Claire. It's a compliment."

"Once you explain it, I guess."

They collected Claire's bags from the luggage carousel. "He

survived the stroke," Maggie said, "but he's worried about his mind."

"Alzheimer's," Claire said. "It's going around."

Maggie shook her head in disbelief. This was certainly Claire, despite all the new refinements.

They drove straight to the hospital.

David was sitting up in bed, looking depressed. "They want me to walk more," he said to Maggie, wondering who the other woman was. Then he recognized his daughter. "Sweetheart!" he said, joyful suddenly. "You look beautiful. Where did you hide the old Claire?"

"So his mind is okay," Claire said to Maggie, "nasty as ever." And to David she said, "Did I look *that* bad before? Don't answer. I thought you were supposed to be dying. Mother said this stroke was the real thing."

"It's the lucky third: all fuss, no lasting damage." And in fact he began once again to feel that he would survive this stroke and walk out of here singing.

SEDGE JOINED THEM in the afternoon. He had driven up from Los Angeles in his little Mazda Miata and arrived with a terrific headache from all the traffic. Sophia, his new fiancée, had wanted to come with him but he persuaded her to wait until he saw what shape his father was in. She could come up for the funeral, he said. So with his headache and his expectations of a dying father, he was not prepared for his newly refurbished sister or his exhausted mother or his not quite moribund father, a man who was supposed to be laid out on a slab. But Sedge's own perpetual optimism and his native good spirits took over and, waving his arms about in that way of his, he said, "I don't know who looks best: my gorgeous mother, my glamorous sister, or my dad who's obviously faking a stroke! What a great family I've got! What a lucky man!"

Everyone was always glad to see Sedge.

WILL ARRIVED THE NEXT DAY and Sedge picked him up at the airport in Maggie's Prius, since his own little Miata was only a two-seater. Sedge knew that Will's marriage had fallen apart and he knew about the graduate student affair but he was not prepared for the startling young beauty of Cloris. She was, of course, blond. She was very tall, taller than Will, and she was at first glance boyishly thin. Her eyes were a deep blue that in some lights looked green and her complexion was that pale English rose. She wore glasses.

"Well!" Sedge said, and his appreciation was evident.

"How is Father?" Will said.

"Very pleased to meet you," Sedge said to Cloris. She looked so English, with that complexion and those great glasses.

"How's Father? Is he going to make it?"

"A mild stroke. He's sitting up and talking."

"This is my fiancée, Cloris," Will said.

"A pleasure," Cloris said.

"You bet," Sedge said. He smiled at her, happy man that he was. "The car is on the third level." He shook his head, making all those black curls tremble, and gestured toward the parking garage. Then, with nothing more to say, he waved his arms about pointlessly. Cloris laughed. "What?" he said. "Tell me."

"I've heard a lot about you," she said.

Sedge let his gaze rest on her a moment longer than necessary while she returned his gaze so that it seemed at this, their first meeting, an understanding was reached.

SO THEY WERE HOME, the whole family, a reunion of caring people. Educated, sophisticated, lacking for nothing. An enviable group.

16.

Reginald Parker visited David early in the morning. He was still eating his breakfast of Honey Bunches of Oats when Reginald poked his head into the room.

"Looking good," Reginald said.

Milk from the cereal ran down David's chin. "Dammit," he said and wiped his chin with the bedsheet.

Reginald reassessed David's condition and said, in a very loud voice, "How are you doing?" He spaced the words so David could understand.

"I've had a stroke," David said, "I haven't lost my hearing."

"Sorry," Reginald said. "I just thought . . ."

"You're probably one of those guys who shout at people who don't understand English."

Reginald knew what he meant.

"To make them understand, I mean. As if noise alone would do it. Oh, shit." He was not making sense. He wondered, and not for the first time, how much damage his brain had sustained. "What am I trying to say?" he asked.

An orderly came in to take the breakfast tray. David greeted him in Spanish, hoping to show Reginald how you speak to people who don't understand English. He repeated his greeting, slightly louder.

The orderly said, "Howdy," and left, annoyed at being addressed in Spanish since he himself was Russian.

David cleared his throat, loudly.

Reginald determined to say nothing until David decided what mood he was in.

"So, how are *you*?" David said finally.

"Claire mentioned that you had had a stroke."

"Claire? My Claire?"

"In an email. She mentioned she would be coming back to Palo Alto because . . ."

"You correspond?"

"Only by email."

"The mode of correspondence was not the question. The question was about the fact of the matter." He was pleased with himself. He had expressed that very well. His mind was not completely gone yet.

"We're friends." Reginald lapsed again into silence, having made his point about Claire.

"Well, that's nice. That's lovely."

More silence.

"Well, you were very good to come."

"My grandmother is dying." Reginald waited for a response. "She's nearly ninety."

"Your grandmother."

"Is dying." David should know this. David should know that he, too, Reginald Parker, was somebody. Somebody, moreover, who was an intimate friend of Claire. He was as good as any of them.

David murmured something polite about the grandmother.

Instantly Reginald felt like a fool. Why had he degraded himself this way? Who cared whether this old bastard recognized that Reginald was somebody? After all, who was the old bastard himself but a second-rate academic with a dysfunctional family? As his novel-in-progress would demonstrate.

Reginald was disgusted with himself and decided he needed a hit of something, at least a little weed.

"Well, I'll leave you to it," he said, and, to conceal his anger, he left the room jingling the coins in his pocket.

David stared at the empty space Reginald had occupied. "I'm sorry to hear about your grandmother," David said, and was surprised that he did indeed feel sorry. It must be the effect of the stroke.

17

At the Hollisses' house there was a general sense of confusion. Rooms and the privacy they provided had been worked out satisfactorily before Will and Cloris showed up, but now with these two extra people life was in turmoil.

Claire had taken up residence in her old room; it had been converted into a study for Maggie but the daybed there served well enough for a short visit. Claire had brought two large suitcases and her many new outfits filled the small, old-fashioned closet. *You can't go home again*, she told herself, at least not when everybody else goes home at the same time. She wanted privacy. Who were all these dreadful people?

Sedge moved into his old room, which served now as a guest room. There were towels on the newly made bed and little bars of scented soap. He dumped these on the bureau. His mother meant well but a grown man needed a real bar of soap. Besides, he hated to cause this fuss.

Will, the Perfect Son, was camping out with Cloris in his old room, which had long since been taken over for storing useless stuff: discarded luggage, lamps and end tables, and, in one corner, piles of books to be donated to the local library. Cloris cheerfully accepted her secondary status in the house, well aware that she was an outsider who was not yet a married member of the family. She was happy just to be included.

"Where do you *put* anything in this house," Will asked Cloris, behaving for the moment as if he were not the Perfect Son. "I need to shower and there's no place to *put* anything and the dresser drawers are full of old curtains. Why do they keep all this junk? End tables and lamps and suitcases. Why don't they give this stuff to the poor?"

There were three bedrooms upstairs but only two bathrooms. This had been fine when the children were young: Claire had her own bathroom and the two boys shared the other. But now with Cloris visiting there had to be some time strategy for Sedge and Will and Cloris to share the toilet and the shower and for Sedge to do his hair. None of them except Cloris was used to living like this, crowded into a small space with all these other bodies and their clothes and their luggage, so when Will asked rhetorically, "Why don't they give this stuff to the poor?" Cloris responded quite reasonably, "What poor?" She was at that moment looking out the window at the manicured lawn and the swimming pool bordered by red and white flowers just coming into bloom.

"Well, there must be poor people somewhere," Will said.

"I think this is very nice," Cloris said. "It's like living in somebody's attic. We can share the bathroom with your brother. It's not that big a deal. Or I could share with Claire."

"Don't mess with Claire. That's always been her bathroom."

Claire had already taken the problem in hand. Her bathroom

had two doors, one opening to her room and the other to the hall. She had simply locked the hall door from inside and in this way created for herself a private bathroom. Will and Cloris could share the other one. With Sedge.

"And Sedge's latest fiancée will be coming soon. What are they going to do about her?" Will was not resigned to sharing.

"I can't wait to get a look at her, a Hollywood star."

"She works in wardrobe. She's not a star."

"All the same. She works in film."

"Sedge is too old for stars. He's never attracted the star type."

"But he's still attractive. That black hair."

Will looked at her with suspicion, thought better of it, and gave her a kiss. Life with the young was a challenge.

THEY VISITED DAVID in relays during the afternoon so that he'd always have company. This had thoroughly exhausted him and left him feeling cross and put-upon. He wanted Maggie, and maybe Dickens, but all these people and all this talk? Dying, by comparison, looked easy. He had to get home soon so they could all go away.

THEY FOUND THE HOSPITAL visits tedious, though none of them would admit to it. They loved their father, and to be there for him and provide him consolation was the least they could do. They agreed on this over lunch and they agreed on it at greater length afterward when they took Dickens for a walk to the park. At the last minute Claire decided not to join them; instead she borrowed her mother's Prius to go and meet a friend for coffee. Will and Cloris and Sedge set off together for a walk with the reluctant Dickens.

"So when do we get to meet the movie star?" Will asked, just to be difficult.

"She works in wardrobe. She won't be coming up. As a matter of fact, I'll be leaving first thing tomorrow. Dad looks to be okay and I should be getting back to the lab. If anything bad should happen—you know, if he gets worse—Mom can call me in LA and I can be here in no time."

"I had hoped to meet a movie star," Cloris said. "What's her name?"

"Sophia."

"And you're going to marry her?"

"We'll probably marry, but it never lasts for more than a couple years."

"What a shame."

"There's a curse on me," he said happily. "I love to be married— I'd love to marry *you*—but it never lasts. I should carry a sign saying 'Two-Year Limit.'"

They all laughed and Dickens turned around to see what was so funny.

"Maybe this one will last," Cloris said.

He shrugged and waved his hands about and shook his black curls. It was a funny little performance and Cloris laughed at him.

"The big thing," Will said, annoyed, "is that we're all here to support Mother and provide Father with some consolation."

"That's the big thing."

"That's the only thing."

CLAIRE WAS LATE getting home because, after an unsettling number of Starbucks lattes, she and Reginald had not been able to agree on where they should go to have sex. His house was out of the question and so was hers. Reginald was all in favor of the back seat of the Prius but Claire said she was forty-three and there was nothing romantic about a Prius and at her age she needed a bed under her, so it was a hotel or nothing. They went to the Stanford Arms and Reginald—with an eye to his coming inheritance— paid the bill, and did so with a sense of satisfaction. He had arrived. But in the end the evening was something less than a total success for either of them and Claire had come home exhausted and unwilling to talk to anybody. Still, she was here to support her mother and she would, dutifully. She'd just put her head in the door, say good night, and then go straight to her room.

Her mother was propped up in bed, reading. "Good night, sweetie," Claire said. "Sleep well."

"Who did you see?" Maggie asked. "Whom?"

"Reginald," Claire said. She owed her mother her customary frankness.

"Parker? The one we had dinner with?"

"The very one."

"I wondered about him. And you." She waited for a response. "Is this to be an ongoing thing?"

"I doubt it. But it's ongoing for the time being."

"And what about Helen? What about Iris?"

"Helen's his wife. Iris is his daughter. I'm just his friend."

"So it isn't a bed thing?"

"Yes, it is a bed thing. But Helen and Iris are not my responsibility. He wouldn't be having a fling with me if there wasn't already something wrong there."

A long silence.

"I find this reprehensible."

"Don't worry yourself, Mother. You're not the one doing it. You're still a model of familial virtue. Nighty night."

Claire closed the door quietly. Frankness was painful. Often.

IT WAS TWO in the morning and Sedge had had a lot to drink and, unable to continue sleeping, he got up to pee. He had tried to sleep through it, but he was late forties now and his bladder was not what it used to be. He hadn't brought a robe but everybody was long asleep so it didn't matter that he was wearing only his boxer shorts. Besides, he was still in good shape.

The bathroom door was closed and he could see light beneath the door. He'd have to wait. Two minutes passed, then three, and he began to get anxious. It was undoubtedly Will in there, having a solemn, meditative poo, but what if it were not Will but Cloris? He'd just have to wait it out. Finally he couldn't wait any longer. He tapped lightly at the door. He listened for some sound and then tapped again. The door opened a crack and Cloris peeped out. She gave Sedge a shy smile and opened the door wide.

"I'm reading," she said. "I've got jet lag."

She was wearing a matching nightgown and peignoir, both of them semitransparent, and her figure no longer looked boyish. Her hair was pulled back in a ponytail. She adjusted her glasses and smiled.

"It's the middle of the night," she said. "I didn't want to wake Will."

"Yes," he said. "What are you reading?"

She held the book out to him. "It's your father's biography of Crane. He's a very good writer. Your father."

"I've never read him."

"It's the middle of the night," she said again. "You probably want to use the bathroom."

"Yes."

They were standing very close. She was beautiful and she was wearing those terrific glasses. Sedge couldn't stand it a minute longer. He leaned forward and put his hands lightly on her shoulders and lowered his face to hers. He kissed her very softly, gently, a fatherly kiss to a girl half his age.

"I had to," he said.

"Yes," she said. "Good night, Sedge." She went slowly to her room.

18.

Maggie was up early getting breakfast for her family. Sedge had left earlier that morning, not even waiting for a cup of coffee. He had to get back to the lab, he said, there was a ton of work to do. Besides, he was useless here. His father would make a better recovery if there was less noise around him. And all these visitors. It was too much.

Maggie understood: he wanted to leave so he left.

She was making a big batch of scrambled eggs. A plate of bacon was cooked and ready to serve once they all came down for breakfast, and there were hot blueberry muffins and toast and coffee. She was so tired she was ready to lie down on the kitchen floor and the day had not even begun.

Cloris came down first and offered to help with breakfast but all the work had been done. "You can pour the orange juice," Maggie said. "You're such a lovely girl."

Claire came into the dining room at just this moment and said, "You *are* lovely, and so young. Are you and Will planning a family? In addition to his three daughters, I mean. He has three or maybe five."

"Claire," Maggie said. "Please try."

"We haven't gotten that far," Cloris said. "We aren't married yet."

"Are you Church of England, like Daphne? They made her have all those children." Before Cloris could answer, Claire went on. "We're not very strong on religion around here. Father is an atheist, more or less, and Mother was some kind of Christian but gave it up for Father's godlessness. I'm the holdout. I almost became a nun."

Cloris was dazzled into silence by this barrage of information.

Will arrived, full of energy after his night's sleep, and gave everyone good-morning kisses. "Has Sedge left?" he asked. "He wasn't in his room when I came down." And to Claire he said, "What's this about becoming a nun?"

Claire repeated her story about the mother superior and the Little Sisters of the Poor. She had honed it to a fine point by now and it made a nice comic set piece. Will laughed appreciatively.

"And where is Sedge, did you say?"

Maggie explained that Sedge had to go back to Los Angeles.

"What does he do, actually?" Cloris asked.

"Research." They all said it together. It was the one thing everybody knew about him.

"On what?" Cloris asked, but nobody knew, except that whatever it was, it took place in a laboratory and was for the good of mankind.

It was a lazy breakfast and they sat around afterward drinking coffee.

"We should go see Father," Will said finally.

"Frankly, unless somebody's dying, hospital visits are a roaring bore."

"Claire!" Maggie said, appalled.

"I'm just saying something we all know. Let's be frank."

They decided to visit David in relays once again so there would always be someone with him.

Claire said she would go later. She wanted to help her mother clean up after breakfast. Poor Misery. She wasn't good at handling frankness.

edge had left for Los Angeles on Tuesday morning, the chaste kiss with Cloris still warm on his lips, and he returned on Friday morning, early, before everyone was up. When Maggie appeared in the kitchen to start preparing breakfast, Sedge was bent studiously over his coffee with Dickens curled up at his feet. He was worried about Dad, he explained, and Maggie said of course and gave him a kiss and wondered what might be the real reason for his return home.

"How is he doing?" Sedge asked.

She gave him the brief version. There had been no further strokes and no likelihood of one. The handsome doctor said there was an eighty percent chance David would live out his life in perfect health, or at least stroke-free, which would be welcome news if only David were a statistic and not an individual person. He was in good spirits except when he was surrounded by visitors and he was desperate to come home and enjoy a little privacy.

"And how are you?" she asked. "And how is the movie star?"

"She's not a movie star. She's in wardrobe. And we broke up."

They had broken up when it became clear to Sophia that Sedge was not joking about his marriages being cursed with a two-year limit. Here they were, barely engaged, and already, over this past weekend, she could sense a loss of interest on his part. She feared that two months rather than two years might be the limit. Sedge insisted at first that what she sensed was his worry over his father, but after those first feeble protests, he gave up and said she was right, he was a coldhearted bastard and she should move on to a happier life with someone who wasn't cursed. He reported all this to Maggie as if she were his new girlfriend instead of his mother.

"It would have been nice," he said.

"For two years at most," Maggie said, relieved.

They smiled at each other, devoted mother and wayward son. Sedge helped her prepare the breakfast.

Claire was the first to appear. She had on a yellow pantsuit, cut low in front and fitted to perfection. Her hair was combed and fluffed into that new becoming halo. She wore light summer makeup. Her transformation was still a source of wonder to Maggie and now to Sedge as well.

"May I say that I like having a new and very glamorous sister?"

"You may say it as often as you like."

"I'll say it again. You look terrific, Claire."

"You've always been my favorite brother."

"You look ten years younger."

"I feel ten years younger."

"Lucky Willow," he said.

Maggie could not help herself. "Peace in our time," she said. "If only David were home to see it."

Dickens thumped his tail against the floor. He was in pain early in the morning but he did his best to show enthusiasm when it was required.

Will came into the kitchen, full of good spirits. "Sedge!" he said. "What a nice surprise!"

"The Perfect Son," Sedge said. "And here we all are. The perfect family."

Cloris joined them in the kitchen. She wore jeans and a sweatshirt, with her hair pulled back in a ponytail.

"Sorry to be the last one down," she said.

"You're not a morning person," Claire said.

"I am actually."

"She is actually," Will said.

"Actually," Claire said. "Ek-chu-ally."

"What's that supposed to mean?" Sedge was annoyed.

"I'm making fun of Will," Claire said. "The Perfect Son is turning Brit."

"There are worse ways to turn," Will said.

"Meaning?"

"Meaning lesbian."

"Oh, for God's sake, Will. She didn't *turn* lesbian. She *is* lesbian. Get used to it." Sedge felt he had to defend his poor sister, especially now when she was taking such care to be attractive.

"I'm not merely lesbian, I'm bi. I'm also a mother. Remember Gaius?"

"Claire has wide interests," Maggie said. "Claire is not to be categorized."

"Now, that's sheer bitchery," Claire said.

"Leave Claire alone," Sedge said. "You're always down on her, Mother."

"Sorry. Sorry. If you wait a minute, I'll go kill myself."

"Christ!" Claire said. "Why do I bother!"

There was silence for a while in the wake of the shattered peace. Dickens whimpered from beneath the table.

"I am actually a morning person," Cloris said, and Sedge gave her a broad smile. She was wearing those great glasses.

20.

They agreed once again to visit David in relays while Maggie was left to relax and shop for food and supervise the weekly housecleaner. She deserved a rest. Besides, she was committed to her afternoon visit with little Iris, who seemed to have a daily appointment with Maggie that could not be compromised, she made clear, except perhaps by death. So. They would take turns visiting the old man.

Claire chose the first shift so she could be free for lunch with Reginald.

David, captive and resigned, seemed annoyed from the start, and Claire could see it would not be easy to cheer him up. She asked about his book on Gissing but that only seemed to annoy him further. He stared ahead, silent. She talked about Iris and what a remarkable little girl she was and how much she seemed to love Maggie but that, too, was met with silence. Boring. A roaring bore. Desperate, Claire considered telling him about her brisk fling with Reginald but feared he might have another stroke. Luckily they were interrupted by an orderly bearing David's pills on a little china plate. "Time for your goodies," he said, "lucky you!" They were grateful for the interruption. "What a lovely little plate," Claire said. The orderly said, "I always think pills taste better when they're beautifully served." David said, in the orderly's sugary tones, "What a lovely little bunch of pills." And suddenly, for no reason, the tension dissolved and they felt loving and expansive. They chatted with the orderly like an old friend. Just for delivering pills.

"I've got to leave early, Poop," Claire said. "Do you mind being alone like this? I could stay a little longer if you wanted."

"The quiet is nice," David said. "And I've got a lot to think about."

"Love you," Claire said, and she was out the door.

WILL WAS TO HAVE the second shift but he was not due at the hospital for more than an hour so he used this time for a brotherly talk with Sedge. They took Dickens to the park and sat on a bench while the tired old dog curled up at their feet to wait until they'd had enough exercise.

"I need advice," Will said, and then fell silent.

Sedge dithered for a moment. "If it's about divorce, I don't want to talk about it."

"But you must be an expert on it."

"I am." Sedge had given the subject a great deal of thought. "This business of moving from woman to woman is a sign that you don't know yourself. You don't know who you are and you don't know what you're looking for. And I don't want to talk about it."

"But you've been divorced four times."

"Because I don't know who I am and I don't know what I want. Well, I do actually. Talk about something else. Tell me about your work on Yeats."

"You're my big brother. You're supposed to help me. Not by Yeats alone doth man live."

"Here's something. I've always wondered why Keats is pronounced 'Keets' and Yeats is pronounced 'Yates.' Shouldn't it logically be 'Keets' and 'Yeets' or 'Kates' and 'Yates'? There must be a reason."

"That's just how it is," Will said. "What I want to know is when does it end? The guilt and the . . . poor Daphne . . . the guilt."

"I've never felt any guilt. I just move on. It's romance. It's nice."

"And I'm not sure about Cloris."

"Why? Cloris is terrific. She's beautiful and smart and . . ."

"And there's the problem of money."

"There's always plenty of money. Don't disturb yourself."

"Daphne wants to put me in the poorhouse, what with alimony and the mortgage and monthly support for the girls. Christ, I've already spent half the money they sent me to buy a cottage. I felt guilty asking them."

"They'll take it out of your inheritance. They're good about money."

Dickens moaned and shifted from one side to the other.

Will said, "I don't know what to do. Give me some advice."

"Will. I don't want to offend you, seeing you're the perfect son and all, but I wonder if you know what you really want."

"I *think* that I think Cloris is what I really want."

"She's half your age. She's half my age. And she wears glasses." He barely paused before adding, "All that aside, I can see why you might want to marry her. I'd marry her myself."

"I want a good marriage. Isn't that what we all want? Really?"

"What we *really* want, whether or not we know it, is a marriage like Mom and Dad's, where love for each other excludes the kids." Will stared at him, speechless. "Nothing personal. That's just how they are. But that's why you and Claire are so fucked up."

"And what about you?"

"I'm fucked up, too. The difference is that I know it."

Will said, "But they gave us everything when we were kids."

"Everything but love. They kept that for themselves. It's fine. It's nothing personal, really. Think about it. What they gave us then is what we give them now. A half-assed kind of love."

"I can't believe you're saying this. They were the perfect parents."

"They're very good people. Very good."

"They loved me. They love my kids."

"It's not about you, Will. They're just devoted to each other." Sedge waved his hands and shook his head. "They're the reason I never had kids."

"I thought you liked kids."

"Other people's. I like that Iris kid. And so do they. In fact—and I find this interesting—they love her. In that parental way they never loved us."

"Iris?" Will felt stupid. "Iris? Really?"

"Iris."

As if he had been summoned by the mention of Iris, Reginald Parker suddenly approached their bench. "Dickens," he said, "good old Dickens," and after he gave Dickens a good scratch behind the ears, he said, "I'm Reg Parker, Iris's father. And you must be Will and Sedge."

"I'm Will, the fucked-up brother, and this is Sedge, the other one."

"Well," Reginald said. "How about that."

"Actually," Sedge said, sounding a lot like Cloris, "*actually*, we're about to head for home."

They walked home side by side, the perfect son and the other one, while Reginald trailed behind them with downhearted Dickens on his leash.

SINCE CLAIRE HAD MADE her getaway with the Prius, Will and Sedge and Cloris drove to the hospital in David's ancient Buick. "This thing is great," Sedge said. "It's like riding in a time capsule." The walk had filled him with energy and high spirits and he kept up a lively conversation with Cloris. She listened, fascinated, as he leaned forward from the back seat with his chin set firmly against her headrest. She smelled of lilies and honey, he told her. She was irresistible, he told Will. He loved riding in this old Buick. He loved being with Will and Cloris. He loved going to the hospital to see his father.

Sedge volunteered to wait in the cafeteria while Will and Cloris had their visit with David. "Oh, God," Will said, depressed. Then Cloris said it might be a good idea if she waited in the cafeteria, too, with Sedge, so that Will could have private time with his father. "Oh, God," Will said again. "I can't bear it."

"Be the perfect son," Sedge said. "Give him a good laugh."

"Just be yourself," Cloris said, "tell him about your new book."

Will watched them go and he wondered, not for the first time, if poor abandoned Daphne would take him back.

David was sitting up in bed with his eyes closed, drowsing. "Father," Will said, a bit louder than necessary.

His father, startled and awake, offered Will a big smile. "The Perfect Son," he said. "All the way from England. With Daphne, right? And the girls?"

They had been through all this several times. Had he lost it completely?

Will cleared his throat and said, "With my wife-to-be. Cloris. Cloris will join us later. She's having coffee with Sedge so we can have private time."

"What larks! As Claire would say."

"Claire got that from you. Or Mother."

"From Dickens, I should think. That's where it comes from."

"Dickens," Will said.

"Charles Dickens. Not the dog."

"Dickens."

Silence. Suddenly everything seemed hopeless. They were all fucked up . . . Claire with her acting and Sedge with his marriages and Dickens with his larks and Daphne, poor betrayed Daphne, sorrowing in Essex . . . dear God!

"We should talk about Yeats," Will said, determined to get through the hour. "I've run into some technical problems with the runes."

"Runes? In Yeats?"

"I could use your informed opinion."

"I don't have an opinion on Yeats, informed or otherwise."

"Then I guess it's up to me," Will said.

For the next hour he provided his father with a lot of information about traditional Yeats scholarship, about runes, about throwing out the old scientific reading of the texts. It was a truly terrible hour for both of them.

"So what do you think?" Will asked.

"I've had a stroke," David said. "My brain can't take it in."

Will fell into a sulk. He was tempted to say what he had been thinking all along. He sneaked a quick look at his watch— where was that fucking Sedge?—and then he said it. "Perhaps if I were Iris you could take it in." He was glad he had said it even though he was ashamed of himself. "Since she matters so much to you and Mother."

David smiled and closed his eyes. All that yammering about

Yeats. And Iris? Did he mention Iris? He slept while Will stared at him in despair.

CLORIS AND SEDGE WERE having coffee in the cafeteria. Sedge was talking nonstop to Cloris, who paid no attention to the words he was saying. She was simply enthralled by the performance.

Sedge had never had to seduce anybody. All his wives and even his incidental affairs had fallen to him without effort on his part. He waved his hands and shook his black curls and they were his. Cloris, long denied any company but that of academics, felt certain she had never been so lavishly entertained. Sedge was an intellectual holiday, ageless, and oddly handsome. He talked nonsense and she couldn't get enough of it. She was tired of being cautious and she was terrified at the thought of being a faculty spouse and stepmother to three young girls. And so here she was about to seduce Sedge, the family menace with the two-year marriage curse. Happily dizzy, she reached forward and put her hand on his, lightly, barely touching.

"Your little hand," he said. "Your little academic hand on mine," and he covered them with his free hand, making a nice little amorous pile. A warm minute passed. "This is only romance," he said, sad about it. "We can't make it more than that."

"Romance," she said.

"If Will doesn't mind."

"Lovely Will," she said. "He's still in love with Daphne."

"And you?"

"I'm in love with Will. I think. More or less." She took off her engagement ring and slipped it into her pocket. "He's a very good scholar."

"You're a wonder," he said. "It's those glasses you wear."

"It's your . . . I don't know," she said.

They clasped hands across the table.

"This isn't about sex," Sedge began. "At least not yet." He went on for some time, noting once again the two-year curse on all his marriages and his admiration for—and aspiration to—the ideal marriage of his mother and father and what a perfect son Will had always been, up until now, and how important it was that Will not feel betrayed. They were honorable people. They would do the honorable thing.

By the end of the hour they had convinced themselves they were in love. Sedge and Cloris. Cloris and Sedge.

Now if only Will could be reasonable about this.

MAGGIE SPENT HER MORNING doing housework, ordering groceries, and in general tidying up after a family that had complete control of her life but no control of their own. Only David understood. What luck that they had found each other. And what luck that in their old age they had found the perfect child—well, grandchild—in little Iris. She suspected she loved Iris more than her own children but that would be a terrible thing. She just felt grateful they had Iris in their lives. Thank God. Or Somebody.

———

MEANWHILE CLAIRE WAS HAVING lunch with Reginald at Burger Heaven. He was a vegetarian only when he ate at home, he explained, because eating out had a social dimension that allowed for meat. Especially a burger. Claire nodded agreement because frankly she didn't give a damn. She had bigger things to think about than the ethical problem of eating burgers. She could not get her mother's bitchery out of her mind, and when she tried to focus on Reginald she thought only of how dissatisfying she had found the sex of the previous evening. Reginald, however, both then and now, was happily preoccupied with his grandmother's imminent death.

"She's gonna leave me the whole deal," he said. "The property, the house—wreck though it is—and all that nice money."

"You'll probably give it away, though, so you can walk in the way of the Lord, right?"

He scarcely heard her.

"As a matter of fact, you've never explained how you reconcile our screwing parties with your devotion to the Lord."

"What?" He was brought back suddenly from the consoling reverie of his grandmother's demise to this lunch table at Burger Heaven. And Claire. He hadn't enjoyed their sexual encounters and he blamed her. Cold bitch. Lesbian. How had he ever gotten involved with Claire? And why? "What?" he said again.

"Walking in the way of the Lord. How do you reconcile this with adultery?"

"You don't understand," he said. "It's not about laws. It's about your interior disposition. '*Ama et fac quod vis*,' Augustine says. 'Love and do what you want.' That's the real way of the Lord. Love and justice." Forgetting how annoyed he was with her, he developed his ideas of love and justice at some length—a living wage, your brother's keeper—and he did this without any sense of irony.

Somewhere along the way Claire stopped listening because quite frankly she was not interested in his phony arguments and in fact she was not interested in him. Reginald was just like her mother, always having it both ways. Her perfect marriage and her bitchery to Claire. Her love for her husband and distinterest in her children. That's what it meant for these fakers to walk in the way of the Lord. Some walk. Some Lord.

Reginald had finished with the Lord by now and so Claire started in on her mother. She was selfish, she was mean in her every thought and word, she was anti-lesbian. She was a compound of all things hypocritical and frankly her scrambled eggs were always overdone. Besides, besides . . .

"Go ahead," he said. "Be frank."

This was one thing that could distract Reginald from Granny's coming death: more dirt on the Holliss family to use in his novel.

"Tell me about it," he said to Claire. "Tell me everything."

He had no way of knowing that at this very moment in leafy, faux rustic Hillsborough, his grandmother pulled herself together and, taking a deep breath, turned toward the sunny window and, altogether satisfied, passed to her eternal reward, leaving her grandson nothing or next to nothing.

"Tell me everything," Reginald said again, greedy as always for tales of truth and justice.

DAVID HAD DRIFTED OFF to sleep during the last of Will's lectures on Yeats and now, with the arrival of Cloris and Sedge, he had begun to snore.

"We had a great coffee, Will," Sedge said. "Cloris is the greatest girl."

"He's lovely," Cloris said. "He's everything you've always said."

Will was uncertain what to make of this since he had always said his brother was a shit. Period.

David stopped snoring and opened his eyes. He saw Will standing there watching Cloris and Sedge, who looked to David's educated eye to be in some kind of sexual thrall and he couldn't stand it a moment longer. "Go!" he shouted. "All of you! Let me have my stroke in peace!"

The three of them stepped out into the corridor to discuss what they should do. Call a nurse? Call a doctor? Go away, as requested?

Sedge put his head in the door and looked at David, who was lying there quietly with his eyes shut and his hands folded on his chest, as if he were waiting for the welcome advent of an easy death.

"He looks so peaceful," Sedge said. "Why not just let him be?"

They all went home to see how Maggie was getting on. This stroke business was hardest of all on her, they supposed. He was all she had.

———

DAVID HAD A LIGHT TIA that evening, a kind of mini-stroke that the handsome doctor dismissed as meaningless. These things happened and they didn't matter at all. Except sometimes when they did.

"It's a function of age," he said. "You've earned the right to a free TIA." He clapped David on the shoulder and assured him he could be home before the end of the week. "Good news," he said. "Nothing but good news."

21

S edge had put off his talk with Will until dinner was over and Maggie had left for her private visit with David—no kids allowed—and Cloris had decided on a good long soak in the bath.

"Let's take a walk," Sedge said.

"Dickens has had his walk," Will said. "And I don't want one."

Dickens thumped his tail once and gave a sigh.

"It's just that we should talk."

And so they walked and talked. Or rather Sedge talked and Will listened, with disbelief initially but with a growing sense that he was trapped by fate. This truly was outrageous. Cloris and Sedge? Sedge and Cloris? Will was—there was no other word—outraged. Talk about duplicity! Talk about betrayal! You had to go back to Greek tragedy to find a brother seducing his brother's wife! Fiancée, rather. Will raged on and on and Sedge listened, suppressing the desire to ask which Greek tragedy Will had in mind. Wasn't this more like a soap opera? Except of course this was real, this had already happened, this was about them. And Will had a point.

"You're right, Will. It's unspeakable," Sedge conceded, but

Will raged on. He was exhausted finally and, giving in to the inevitable, said, "Well?"

For the next twenty minutes Sedge presented a rational, detailed, and pragmatic account of his incipient romance with Cloris: they couldn't help themselves, it simply happened, the question was, What Now?

Will launched into a further burst of outrage, but the heart had gone out of him by now, and after a third outburst, Sedge managed to repeat, "You're right, of course, Will, you're absolutely right." Will muttered something about betrayal and murder, but Sedge explained, "It's just infatuation at the moment, but it promises to have all the staying power of my former marriages."

"Two years, you mean."

"At the most."

"And what am I supposed to do? Wait around for two years until she leaves you and decides to come back to me?"

"That's a crass way to put it, but as a matter of fact . . ."

"When did all this start, anyway? You've only just met her."

"It's simple, Will. It started very innocently on the night you arrived. She had jet lag and was reading Dad's book on Crane and I kissed her—it was a very chaste kiss, truly—in the hallway outside the bathroom. And then we both went our ways. Just a brotherly kiss."

"Jesus!"

"I don't know why you're so surprised. I told you when I first met her—I told you both—that I'd marry her in a minute. She's a beauty. And with those glasses!"

"I should phone Daphne and see how she's doing."

"Just so you don't feel betrayed. Cloris and I wouldn't want that."

"Daphne says she's mindless. Daphne says our marriage won't last a year. Cloris and me."

"Maybe Daphne knows something. Maybe our whole family carries the marriage curse. A one-year limit for you. Two for me. Six months for Claire."

"Poor Daphne." Will sighed in resignation. "Poor Bartleby."

"Who's Bartleby?"

"Honest to God! You're illiterate. The whole modern world is illiterate."

"But are you all right?"

"I didn't know I was cursed, too."

In this way, with consideration of the marital curse and the illiteracy of the modern world, they wore themselves out. Will was for the present drained of his rage. Sedge's sense of betrayal had scaled down to mild embarrassment. By the time they reached home, the sky was beginning to get dark and the moon came up and they were relieved that it was almost over. Whatever it was.

22.

The handsome doctor phoned that night to tell Maggie of David's TIA. "Nothing to worry about. We'll just keep watch." So Maggie informed each of them that there would be no visiting David tomorrow. He needed rest. He needed peace. They had been sobered and solemn as they went off to bed.

Now they were gathered together for a family breakfast and everyone had a dismal headache. Maggie had made a great stack of pancakes and a plate of bacon and there was plenty of coffee. She put the pancakes and bacon in the middle of the table and said, "I'm done," in that tone she used when she was in a dangerous mood. Nobody spoke for a while.

"I love American breakfasts," Cloris said into the silence. "They're so minimal."

Maggie froze, her fork poised above her plate.

"Delicious, I mean," Cloris said, "but without a lot of distracting things like tomatoes and baked beans and burnt bread."

"English breakfasts are poisonous," Claire said. "A cup of coffee is all anybody needs." She smiled at her mother and took another pancake. "You're a good cooker, Misery."

"I didn't mean . . ." Cloris said.

"Let's talk about something safe," Will said, "let's talk about money."

Everybody looked at him.

"Nobody should ever talk about money," Sedge said.

"Not first thing in the morning," Claire said.

"My money, you mean." Maggie corrected herself: "You mean *our* money. David's and mine."

"Well, we're all going to inherit it . . . eventually . . . and I could use some now." He examined his plate closely. "I phoned Daphne last night and she's willing to consider taking me back but she made it clear that it's going to cost me." He was afraid to look up. "And I've already put down fifty thousand pounds on that cottage for me and Cloris and I'm going to forfeit that when I withdraw my offer, so I'm in a financial bind." He looked up at their amazed faces. "I think now is a good time to talk about what we'll eventually get." Silence. "I'd like to draw on a little of my share."

"You always were the Perfect Son," Maggie said.

"You really are the perfect shit," Claire said. "At a time like this? With Misery and Poop on the edge of the big Never Never? How could you? You could at least wait till they're dead. God! Anyhow they'll leave us equal shares the way they always planned. Right?" She looked at Maggie. "Or whatever they de-cide. It's their money."

"There's just the three of us," Will said. "I'm only saying."

"But then there's Iris," Maggie said. "Don't forget Iris."

"Iris?" Will said.

"Iris!" Claire said.

Sedge began to hum softly. He didn't care about money. In his experience money was best not thought about. They listened to his humming.

"American bacon is very different to English bacon," Cloris said.

"Different *from*," Claire said.

"Different *to*," Cloris said, and for a second that beautiful lower lip curled down in anger. "It's a matter of choice and I'm English and I choose *to*."

Sedge looked at her in surprise. Sweet, shy Cloris could hold her own. There was always more to women than you bargained for.

Claire said, "There are good choices and poor choices."

Maggie said, "I don't think it's good form to argue about grammar at the breakfast table." She rose slowly. "Please rinse your dishes and put them in the dishwasher when you're done. I'm off to visit my husband in the hospital."

She left but then came back for a moment. "And when you walk Dickens, whoever does it, make sure you take a plastic bag to pick up his poo."

WILL VOLUNTEERED TO TAKE DICKENS for his walk. The park was just a large rectangle of stubbly grass dotted here and there with dog poo and a couple of benches for you to sit on while you waited for your dog to do his business. Will hated the park but somebody had to be responsible and he, after all, as the Perfect Son, et cetera, et cetera. He had thought Cloris might join him—anything is possible—but she had other plans for the day. With Sedge.

Beautiful, nearsighted Cloris, who only a year ago had been a different person. "You're the perfect husband, Mr. Holliss," Cloris had said to him after first meeting Daphne, and "You're the perfect father, Will" after seeing him with his daughters. "You're all I ever imagined, darling." But by then they had become lovers. Their relationship had been complicated by the fact that Cloris had finished her coursework and for the past two years had been reading the Bloomsbury Set in hopes of finding a thesis topic that had not yet been exhausted by the Woolf industry. She had read the Woolf canon, both Virginia and Leonard. She had read all of Keynes and Forster and Strachey. She had read the endless related biographies and criticism. The Set was thrilling and suffocating at the same time, and she loved reading about them, but she could find nothing new to say. The Bloomsburys were—at least for her—spent. "I can't do this," she said one day in a sudden burst of tears, and Will, who had long been convinced she was right, lied and said, "Of course you can. I'll help you. You're just nearsighted." Cloris, however, held on and said, "No, I like reading books but I have nothing to say about them. I'm not an academic and I never will be." There was a long silence while Will dealt with her tears. "Marry me, then," he said, and Cloris said, "Yes. And yes."

And now she was off with Sedge for the day and he was left with brokenhearted Daphne, who might or might not take him back and, at the moment, with a dog who wouldn't poo.

Cloris and Sedge! Who would believe it?

He consoled himself that he alone among the three Holliss offspring had made an intellectual and social success of his life. He was a respected scholar and the father of three lovely girls and . . . who could say . . . soon he would once more be a loving and dutiful husband . . . hopefully . . . once Daphne got over this punitive state she was in. Dear, devoted Daphne. For the time being, she had said, he could live in the little attic room above the garage. He was convinced, however, that when he had done sufficient penance and their old kitchen was completely renovated—she had insisted on this—he would be allowed to move back into the house. He had promised that they would spend next summer in Majorca, if they could afford it. He could borrow the money if he didn't have it at the ready, she said. And . . . and. Obviously Daphne had thought all this through and would be the dutiful put-upon faculty spouse no longer. Furthermore, she said, they needed a new downstairs bathroom. At once.

Will felt as desolate as the dog park itself.

Dickens, sympathetic to the end, did his poo and they turned for home.

SEDGE AND CLORIS SPENT the day at Stanford Shopping Center, with visits to the jewelry trays at Shreve and at Gleim and for lunch at La Baguette, the little outdoor café in the courtyard. It was a perfect day for two lovers.

At Shreve they found the loveliest engagement rings Cloris

had ever seen, but they were chiefly diamond solitaires and Sedge, thinking back to his many previous engagements, said perhaps they looked too traditional. They examined different kinds of rings—diamond with sapphires, diamond with emeralds—but Sedge seemed to lack the enthusiasm that would convince Cloris to choose. So they sauntered hand in hand for a leisurely coffee at Starbucks to diminish their ocular dazzle before taking on Gleim.

"Poor Will," Cloris said. "I feel bad for him."

"Not to worry. Will is a born scholar. He still has Yeats. And maybe Daphne."

"But he's walking the dog while we're shopping for an engagement ring."

"Will likes the dog."

"It's a sweet dog. But still . . ."

"Think of your ring. We've got to get you something fabulous."

"But all this money! Perhaps we shouldn't."

"There's always money. Everyone has money."

"So we're off to Gleim?"

"Gleim is different to Shreve. You'll love it."

"Different *to*. You're the sweetest man." She kissed his cheek.

They had found nothing that would do in Gleim until, on their way out, they stopped at a desolate tray of estate jewelry and in the center of the tray discovered—instantly and together—the perfect ring. It was a triple band of diamonds, the stones graduated in size, and on Cloris's finger the ring seemed a slash of light in many soft, alluring colors.

Two years and maybe more, Sedge said to himself, and to Cloris he said, "I think this is *you*."

Cloris, a dedicated romantic, said, "This is *us*."

The magic moment was not at all spoiled when Sedge had to shuffle through his credit cards for the one that was not overdrawn. He found it and happily charged another ten thousand dollars on American Express.

He slipped the ring on her finger and, her palm against his heart, she gave him a small, public kiss. No matter. They would spend the next four hours in the bridal suite of the Stanford Park Hotel.

CLAIRE WAS ASTONISHED as she and Reginald came out of the Stanford Park Hotel to see Sedge and Cloris checking in.

"This is where we greet one another as old friends," Claire said, "instead of pretending we've never met. California is different to England." She gave Cloris her frank smile, an offer of goodwill. After all, Cloris might well be the next sister-in-law.

"You're being terribly nice about this," Cloris said. "It's embarrassing."

"Life's embarrassing. You've got to face it head-on."

"I love Americans. You're all so uncomplicated."

"Frankly . . ." Claire said, but decided not to go on.

The two men shuffled back and forth, uncomfortable.

"Sedge," Reginald said.

"Reginald," Sedge said.

"Your room is ready," the desk clerk said, amused, and not the least bit uncomfortable.

MAGGIE AND DAVID were alone at last. The doctor had made his promised visit, the nurse had stopped by to make sure the doctor had visited as promised, the giddy orderly had come in with his plate of pills, and now there was peace and a little privacy.

Maggie sat on the side of the bed and laid her head on the pillow next to his. "My sweetheart," she whispered. "How are you? In yourself."

"Terrified," he said. "But I still have you."

She gave him a gentle kiss.

"I've been thinking," he said.

"I know," she said.

"I've been thinking about my atheism. I think it indicates a closed mind. I'm considering the possibility of agnosticism."

"It's the TIA talking."

"Probably. But I'm serious. If you don't believe in God, why get so excited about him. Or her. Or it. Would you love me more if I were an agnostic?"

"I love you exactly as you are. You don't have to give up atheism for me."

"I believe in you and that's enough." He pulled her closer.

"I adore you," she said.

She snuggled up against him and kissed his ear. The hairs in it needed trimming. There was always something.

"We'll have a lovely day," she said. "Everything is wonderful here at the hospital."

So they had lunch together and took a long nap and then she went to the cafeteria and brought back hot fudge sundaes for dinner. It was the hospital, yes, but they were together and it was a kind of paradise.

Now if only the children would leave.

23.

David would be coming home any day now and Maggie couldn't wait. She had the weekly housecleaner in for an extra session and she had stocked the freezer with David's butter pecan ice cream and she had picked up his prescriptions for Plavix and Vytorin. She was all ready, if only the children would decide to leave, she said.

"After all, we're old people now. We can't be running a hotel for the insane at our age. We're approaching eighty."

"We're seventy-four. We just feel eighty."

"And I look eighty."

"You look beautiful. Send them all home."

Maggie had asked the family not to visit the hospital today so that she and David could be alone to plan his convalescence.

"Where did we go wrong?" she said. It was not a question. "Will always seemed the perfect son."

"They're all perfect for a while and then suddenly they're not."

"We did everything we could. Did we?"

"Send them all home. The perfect with the imperfect."

"They love us, in their way."

In fact they were all eager to be gone. Claire had run out of good times with Reginald and longed once again for the creative chaos of the repertory theater. Sedge wanted only to be alone with Cloris. And the Perfect Son was just waiting for the proper moment to say goodbye to his father and his mother and his former fiancée since Cloris was now so dizzily in love with Sedge. They were planning an autumn wedding.

THEY WERE GATHERED in the living room on the night before David's return home. Dinner had been civil enough. Claire had restrained her need to be frank and Will remained too numb to express his fury and dismay. Sedge and Cloris sat side by side on the love seat, her little hand in his.

Maggie had put out drinks for anybody who wanted a night-cap but nobody was interested. There was a lot of silence in the room.

"Blessed quiet," Maggie said. "What a relief."

"It's gonna be a great two years." Sedge tossed his head from side to side, shaking out his black curls. "This is a promise."

"Two years for starters," Cloris said.

"Good luck with that," Claire said. "They may be the longest two years of your life."

"I'm the exception," Cloris said. "The curse won't work on the Brits. Actually."

"I wonder when Daphne will let me back in the house," Will said to no one in particular. "I miss the girls."

"Ek-chu-ally," Claire said.

Dickens was lying at Maggie's feet. He gave a great sigh.

"This is surreal," Maggie said. "I wish your father was here." No one responded so she went on. "I sometimes think I've gone mad and am just hallucinating about the lives of my children, that none of this could really be happening. I think back to when you were little and what mattered most to us, to David and me, was your health and your happiness. And here you are now in your forties, scattered all over the face of the earth and utterly miserable, with all these odd men and women coming and going in your lives. You need a chart to remember who's married to whom. You were all so sweet as children and look what you've grown up to be. It's awful."

"That's typical Maggie," Claire said to Cloris. "You'll get to see a lot more of this in your two years in the family. She hates us. She doesn't hate you yet because she doesn't know you yet—actually—but give her time and you'll see, you'll see." She got up and poured herself a scotch and water.

"I don't think we've turned out so bad," Sedge said. "We've all got good jobs and we lead responsible lives and for the most part we don't drink. I just happen to get married a lot."

"I don't," Will said. "I was married only once and I'm going back to it. To Daphne. If she'll have me."

"Of course she'll have you," Cloris said. "Daphne is a lovely woman. Besides, she's meant to be married to an academic. She's that kind of woman. I'm not. Thank God I discovered that before it was too late."

"Thank God I discovered you," Sedge said. "Late or not." He lifted her hand and kissed her knuckles one by one.

"I may vomit," Claire said. "Does anyone else need a drink?"

No one needed a drink. Claire shrugged and clinked the ice in her glass.

"I think of little Iris and how she's being raised in an insane family and how smart and ladylike she is and I wonder if it's even possible to know how to raise a family today," Maggie said. "Good children grow up to be criminals and the ones who are neglected turn out to be good. It's a mystery. Now take Iris. She has Reginald for a father and . . ."

"Reginald is a shit," Claire said. "To be absolutely frank."

They all turned to her, expecting more.

"What?" Claire said.

"Well, tell us," Maggie said. "Does this mean the thing between you is a thing of the past?"

"He's writing about us. He's ditched his philosophical novel and he's writing an academic satire. My guess is that he's writing about you. Us."

"An academic satire?" Will asked. "He'll be up against David Lodge and he won't stand a chance."

"I'm sure there's nothing sufficiently interesting about us to put in a novel," Maggie said, and then she thought of Sedge and Cloris and the two-year curse. "A short story, perhaps, but not a novel."

"Well, you may feel different when you see it." Claire did not mention where Reginald had gotten his information.

"I doubt we'll ever see it," Maggie said. "He's not the publishing type."

"Meaning?"

"He'll never finish anything. Just look at him." And she dismissed the topic altogether as too silly to think about. "What worries me is Iris. She's smart and loving and a perfect little child despite the mother and father."

"Has she written you and asked to borrow money?"

"Claire! What a thing to say!"

"Well, has she? Because if she hasn't already, she will. Reg is determined."

"Determined to do what?"

"To use Iris to get at your money."

"But we have no money to loan." Maggie bit her tongue.

"You do have money. You're just not loaning it. At least not to Reginald."

"Reginald has borrowed money in the past, but I'm sure he would never put his daughter in that kind of position."

"He feels the whole world has conspired against him and he wants payback."

"I didn't think he cared about payback." Maggie had still not told David that Reginald returned only two of the four hundred dollars he'd borrowed. "Anyway we've solved that problem," she said.

"What problem?"

"Reginald borrowing money."

"Forget the money. He's borrowing your lives."

"What are you talking about, Claire?"

"The book. The book he's writing."

"Oh, that. I've already told you. There'll never be a book. Now can we talk about something else? Can we talk about your father, who'll be coming home tomorrow? Could we give some thought to that?"

Everybody fell to thinking about David.

"He's still awfully frail, I think," Will said. "Having a stroke reminds you that you're finite and you can lose everything in a second and have nowhere to turn." He looked over at Cloris and Sedge. "As if we need reminding."

"He's still got a lot of life in him," Claire said. "A lot of meanness."

"Claire! How *can* you? Your father loves you so."

"He can't wait until we all go," Claire said.

"*We* can't wait until we all go," Will said.

Everybody looked at him.

"I'm going to go pack," Claire said.

"I'm already packed," Will said.

Sedge and Cloris, caught up in their romance, said nothing.

Maggie looked around at their tired faces. Only her sense of obligation kept this family together. She found herself thinking, *Go! Just go!* but like the good mother she considered herself to be, she said, "He'll miss you all. But he does need his rest."

DAVID RETURNED HOME the next morning and, while the whole family was there to welcome him back, they had all gone their separate ways by noon. David and Maggie and Dickens were at peace at last.

Iris stopped by to visit that afternoon, and that evening they found a message.

Dear Professor and Mrs. Holliss:

    It was lovely to visit you this afternoon and to see Prof. Holliss feeling well again. I missed visiting him during his illness and I missed our reading together.

    I'm writing this email at my father's dictation. He wants you to know this request is from him. Could he please borrow five hundred dollars? The need is urgent or he would not be asking for a loan. He says you will understand this.

    He will stop by tomorrow afternoon.

    Your friend, Iris

And so the time had come to say, "Here. You can regard this as a loan or, if you prefer, as a gift you need never pay back. But however you regard it, this is the last of the money."

It was David's first unpleasant obligation since his stroke and he discharged it firmly and kindly and in the tone of one who traffics in immutable truths. He was clear. He was forceful. And Reginald understood.

PART FOUR

❖ ❖ ❖

24

B y the fall of the year, in September 2010, terrorism had
moved from the great world of international intrigue to the
high schools, to the colleges, to the limitless resources of
the web. Terrorism begins in fear and is impelled by rage and in
the fall of the year 2010 it found its domestic outlet in Face-
book, YouTube, and the persecution of children. Torture, murder, suicides filled the news in Fairfax County and in the
borough of Manhattan, in South Hadley High School and in
Rutgers University, and it thrummed and buzzed through the
great cloud of unknowing that was the internet.

The source of terror at the Parker house was money. There
was the great need for it, the desire to possess it, and any act to
get it seemed to Reginald, in his desperation, to be legitimate
and good. He could think of nothing else. He had the right, the
inalienable right, to his grandmother's money. And now she had
left him nothing, or nearly nothing.

Just before her painless passing, Reginald's grandmother had
amended her will. Reginald's mother inherited lifetime use of
the house in Hillsborough and Reginald inherited the amount
of one year's rent, to be paid out monthly . . . which, he noted,

made it impossible for him to contest her will. At the end his grandmother died knowing she had provided for her own, deserving or not.

To Reginald, however, the year's rent was nothing. She had always provided rent, so she owed him that much at least; and not just rent for one year but for every year for the rest of his life. Helen's pitiful Walmart salary kept them in food and clothes, more or less, but Iris needed her own computer and there were books to buy and eventually she would have to go to college. It crossed his mind that the Hollisses might be willing to pay her college tuition, but he reflected that with any luck the Hollisses would be long dead by then. Still, he reminded himself, they, too, would be leaving money. And why not leave it to Iris instead of to that bunch of losers they had for children? It was the vaguest hope and, on reflection, he recognized that they hated him too much to include his daughter in their will. The encounter with them over the "final" loan of five hundred dollars had told him all he needed to know about their sense of justice. He could have the money, he could keep it, they said, but don't ask for any more . . . ever . . . again.

He had written Claire about the humiliating money scene but she had not answered. She had been all interest and enthusiasm when she was feeding him stories about how screwed up the family was, but she lost her perverse enthusiasm as soon as she guessed that he intended to write not about his family, as he had said, but about hers. And more worrisome still, she was going to be one of the characters. He was disappointed at her bourgeois thinking. Most people would be honored to be included in a novel. Iris Murdoch had done it all the time. People never minded how badly they were portrayed so long as you gave them one admirable characteristic they lacked in real life. He was planning to give Claire great acting talent, something he doubted she really had, despite the play reviews she had shown him. These had been local stuff, puff pieces no doubt, so they didn't really count. Claire would emerge as the one family member with Christian values, even if she herself failed to recognize them as such. The rest of that crowd would get what was coming to them.

At least he'd gotten the five hundred dollars out of them. That was something. They had to be made to pay up, with all their millions in the bank and their grand piano and their swimming pool. And that old fraud lying there by the pool, toasting in the hot September sun, pretending to recover from a stroke. Reginald thought of his visit to the hospital and the milk trickling down David's chin. He had felt a moment of pity for the old bastard until he wiped his chin dry on the bedsheet. Disgusting. He was a disgust. We become in old age even more of what we have always been, a good phrase. He made a note of it. But the money! The money! There must be more money! Lawrence's "Rocking-Horse Winner" came to mind. If only he could buy Iris such a rocking horse. Iris was the key. Iris was the answer to his money problems. Her email had gotten him the five hundred dollars and she would get him a lot more before he was done.

Poor Helen was working herself half to death, asking for extra hours at Walmart, risking the annoyance of her faggoty boss.

"Stop pestering me!" he said to her when she pleaded for extra hours. "You're already at part-time maximum," he said. "Part time means part time and not full time. You're not a full-time employee. You don't qualify, period. Honest to heavens, you people are all the same!" Reginald wanted to know what he meant by "you people" but Helen, wisely, did not inquire. Just thinking about money made him crazy. It was for Iris and Helen that he needed it. He himself could live without it; he had demonstrated that for most of his life. But poor Iris. Poor Helen.

POOR HELEN WAS BORN Helen Driscoll. The time was the 1970s and the place was San Francisco and her parents—Elena and Fred—good friends in marijuana and sometimes in cocaine, were typical druggies of that day and place. They cadged food from the back doors of restaurants and coffee shops, they panhandled down at the wharf, where they also performed— Fred on banjo, Elena singing—and when things got really bad, Elena offered her services as a party escort outside the Jack Tar Hotel on Geary and Van Ness. She hated doing it but it was sheer profit and one trick usually brought in enough cash to keep them going for a week or two. On one of these unprotected forays into amateur prostitution she got pregnant and, after three months of unexplained sickness, she went off to the free clinic where she learned she was going to be a mother. As part of the clinic's service she was warned, firmly, that taking drugs would prove disastrous to the baby. The nurse questioned her about her home, her family, and her feelings about this pregnancy, and when Elena gave only the usual druggie responses, the nurse recommended an immediate abortion. Elena was Roman Catholic, however, and would not even consider it. Instead she left Fred and moved in with her mother, a lawyer and a functioning alcoholic. Elena stopped drugs altogether for several consecutive weeks, and at those times when she absolutely had to have something, she limited herself to marijuana. By the time Helen was born, Elena was thoroughly depressed but she was completely off drugs.

Helen was born prematurely, with only some of the lesser signs of fetal drug addiction. She was tiny at birth and until she was a year old she suffered from a heart murmur. She was hypersensitive to light and sudden noise of any kind and she grew more slowly than other children. She was a pretty little thing and, when Elena tired of life at home and returned to life on the street with Fred, Elena's mother hired a nurse and a nanny and took over the care of the abandoned Helen.

In school she was thought to be slow because, though she was interested and tried hard, she was awkward and frightened and withdrawn. She could not understand jokes and she took sarcasm literally. She had a sweet disposition, however, and tried always to please, and as she grew older she learned how to fit in with the others. Her real life began after high school.

She got a job as a barista at Starbucks. Reginald was a regular there—a super black coffee and a refill—every morning at eleven. He had a favorite easy chair by the window and after the first two weeks he had established his routine and Helen would bring him his coffee without having to take his order. She rarely said anything but she waited on him as if it were a privilege and after some time he noticed that she was pretty.

One morning she brought him his refill and he looked up at her and smiled. She flushed red and returned his smile and she looked beautiful.

"Have you read this?" he asked, and held up his worn copy of *Ulysses*.

"I'm reading it now," she said, and he looked at her as if he didn't believe her. "I am," she said. "I saw you reading it every day and I figured it must be good. So I bought it."

"What do you think of it?"

"I don't understand it. It's very deep, I guess."

"It is deep, and realizing that you don't understand it is the first step to appreciating it."

"I guess," she said.

"It's the greatest novel there is. Period."

"I thought it must be."

The cashier called her then since there were customers waiting.

Helen had with some difficulty learned to concoct every drink on the elaborate menu, and she made them quickly and efficiently and well. She was perfectly happy in her job. But now she had to read *Ulysses* and reading had never come easily to her. She managed to work her way through fifty pages.

"Have you read Mann and Proust?"

"I don't read all that much."

"You should read Mann and Proust. They're the basic modern classics."

"I'm still working on *Ulysses*."

"I'm a novelist myself."

Helen blushed as the conversation turned personal. "I thought so," she said. "I see you writing in your notebook all the time."

"My journal."

"Journal."

"I'm a philosophical novelist, basically."

"It must be wonderful."

He asked her out to the movies.

"What's playing?" she said, and then realized her mistake. "I'd love to," she said.

They went to see *The English Patient* because it was an adaptation from a novel by Michael Ondaatje. The book was well written, Reginald said, but it lacked a sound philosophical base.

"I haven't read it," Helen said.

"You've got a whole education ahead of you." Reginald invited her back to the guest cottage he rented from the Lorings. "We can have a drink in peace there," he said. "It's my new place."

She did not drink, but she accepted his offer to sleep with him. He was pleased to discover she was still a virgin, or had been until now, and he saw happy times ahead. It was easy to see she was hopelessly in love with him.

Later, much later, he was surprised to find he felt something like love for her. He felt protective. He wanted to shield her from her own . . . it wasn't stupidity, really, it was a kind of innocence. He began to ask her questions about herself and was touched to find that her life had been as friendless and unhappy as his own. He asked her more about herself, and still more, and finally said she could move in with him if she wanted. Her natural goodness

198 ❖ JOHN L'HEUREUX

and generosity made up for her mental shortcomings and he found it pleased him to protect her and do things for her. That was why he sometimes made her tea when she came home from work and that was why he loved Iris. They were his family now and—the Hollisses be damned—they were the center of his being, his rock and his salvation. It was for them that he needed money.

HE HAD TO DO something about getting more money. What Helen earned at Walmart was fine, it was good pay for dumb work, but now that he was back smoking—and, to be honest, he did the odd hit of coke as well—there was just not enough cash to go around. It wasn't as if he could take a part-time job at a bar or a fast-food place. That was possible when he was just a druggie but not now that he was a professional writer. He would have to depend on Helen.

Helen, though, had problems. She couldn't go back to Starbucks because she had been fired for theft years ago when she was pregnant. It was just a mistake, really. Reginald had bought a new computer and suddenly they found there was no money for food, not even for the next dinner, so when Helen brought him the change for his coffee, she slipped an extra twenty in with the change. Reginald had promised her it was safe, it was really just a loan and he would pay the money back later, but she was seen doing it and the manager made a note of it. She did it again and another note was made. With the third note, she was confronted with a charge of theft and offered the opportunity to quit. She quit, grateful, but now the best she could do for a job was part time at Walmart.

Reflecting on his money situation, Reginald concluded that it was the Hollisses' fault. They had led Iris into their orbit with cookies and hot chocolate and they had poisoned her mind with gifts of clothing and books and they had pushed their materialistic values on her. They had seduced her away from her own family. They had kidnapped her emotionally. And now they should pay.

This was crazy thinking, he told himself, but it had in it a grain of truth. He made several resolutions.

He resolved to have nothing to do with them. Just let them see Iris as often as they liked until they saw evidence of the harm they had done. Let them see who have eyes to see.

No. He resolved to forbid Iris to see them at all. Once they realized she had cut them off completely, they would come to their senses. They were old, after all, and they were facing death. They needed Iris. She was their connection to life.

No. He resolved to write Claire. She was still crazy for him and he could persuade her that she'd look great as a character in his novel. Or he could just write her out, turn Claire into Clark and make him a handsome rakish gay, cutting a swath through the faggoty wastelands of San Francisco. She'd like that. Ambiguity, she'd call it.

No, it was all hopeless.

He sat at his computer, depressed. It was ten thirty in the evening and his working day was done. There had been the usual agony of writing, with the printer shutting down twice because of paper jams. He had skipped lunch in favor of a walk to the park, but he had seen no sign of Maggie or David: their schedule was a mystery now that the Herr Professor was stroked out. For the first time in ages he had prepared tea for Helen when she returned from Walmart. She was looking worn out, poor Helen. They had had a quiet vegetarian dinner, pasta with tomato sauce, and then, with Iris, they had watched a film on Netflix. He couldn't remember anything about it except that there was constant action that bored him senseless. *The Bourne* Something or Other with that boy from Boston jumping off roofs and beating the crap out of killers with machine guns. Then, while Iris finished her homework, he and Helen had a quiet talk.

"The thing is," he explained, "you have to ask for more hours. Walmart is famous for exploiting their part-time people."

"But I've asked him three times, Reg, Reggie, and he keeps saying I've got as many hours as I'm allowed. If I had more hours I'd be full time."

"I know. I know that." He pulled her closer. "What you have to do is ask him for work off the books. Tell him he can just pay you the minimum wage, and what would ordinarily go to benefits can go to him instead. That way you both make out."

Helen couldn't quite understand this so he repeated himself several times.

"Reg," she said, "Reggie. I couldn't. I don't think I could."

"Of course you can. You're doing it for me and Iris. The thing is not to offend him. You have to pull back if he gets righteous, if he thinks you're offering him a bribe."

"But it is sort of a bribe, isn't it?"

"Good people sometimes have to do bad—equivocal—things."

"Equivocal."

"Equivocal. So you'll do it. Yes?"

"You're a good man, Reggie. I know that." She smiled at him, a little sadly, and for that moment she was beautiful. He kissed her then and told her how lucky he was. He got her a bottle of Ambien to help her sleep.

HE TUCKED THEM IN, first Iris, then Helen, with a chaste kiss for each. His two women. And now he was alone at his computer, depressed, sick with worry about money.

He resolved . . . but, no, he couldn't think of a new resolution. He got up and put on his hoodie and left the house. The sky was overcast and there was no moon, a perfect night for one of his long walks. He would be out of it tomorrow, no doubt, and he would sleep late and lose his writing time, but he had to live, too, you know, he had a right to exist.

He set off with his long loping stride through the dark streets of Professorville. There were all kinds of nightlife in East Palo Alto.

25

D avid was doing well but not as well as expected. He limped a little on his left leg. He was often dizzy and his balance was uncertain. All his gestures were tentative. These things would pass in a short time and, after all, he had suffered a stroke that might have proved fatal. So he was doing well for a man who had had three close encounters with death. This is what he told himself when with difficulty he struggled up from a sitting position or grasped wildly for support as he felt himself about to fall. The earlier strokes had been more kindly and of course he'd been younger then. He didn't fancy himself looking like an old man.

Maggie was very patient with him at first but as days passed and he made excuses for not accompanying her on her slow walks with Dickens, she began to show her impatience.

"You can't just sit there and turn into a vegetable. And you will if you don't start getting out of the house. At least for a walk."

"I'm dizzy, that's all."

"We're all dizzy. Come with me. Dickens has to walk."

"He doesn't want to walk, do you, Dickens. You want to stay here with me."

Dickens thumped his tail against the carpet.

"Dickens is dying. You're not." Tears came to her eyes as she said this. It sounded heartless, and even more so because it was true.

"Well, I don't want to walk but I'll do it if it'll make you happy."

"Happy is a long way from here, let me tell you. Happy will be when you realize you've got to put some effort into living."

And so they walked Dickens, who moved more slowly now and with increasing difficulty.

"See how nice this is?" Maggie said. "You'll feel much better when you get home. You'll have more energy and you'll want to do things. You'll see."

"She's trying to kill me, Dickens," David said.

IRIS STOPPED BY THAT afternoon to say hello and welcome Mr. Holliss home from the hospital and have a cold drink. She had always been much closer to Maggie than to David, but something about his newly discovered weakness made her more attentive to him and she was content to sit for an afternoon while he read to her from *Jane Eyre* and, when he tired, she would read to him. She was caught up in this story of an unwanted girl who grew up to become a governess. She would like to be a governess. She would like to teach school. She wanted to be just like the Hollisses.

She liked best to read with David and then have a little swim in the pool. Maggie had bought her a purple bathing suit, old fashioned with a frilled skirt, and it was kept downstairs in the guest bathroom so she could take a swim without having to carry it to and from home. And since the weather was unseasonably warm she swam nearly every day.

"So long as your parents don't mind," Maggie said.

"My daddy says, 'Whatever makes you happy.'"

David and Maggie found this hard to believe, but there had been no word from Reginald since that final loan of five hundred dollars and they were happy to think that everything was going well for the Parkers. They did not believe it but they wanted to think it was true. So when Iris quoted her daddy saying "whatever makes you happy" they smiled and said wasn't that nice and how very pleased they were. And so was Dickens.

The dog looked up at the sound of his name, but continued to lie stretched out beneath the table.

"Time for a swim," Maggie said, and she and David moved out to the pool while Iris changed into her bathing suit.

"It's too good to be true," David said. "But I like it."

REGINALD WAS DEPRESSED and unable to get on with his novel, but he was careful not to inflict his bad moods on Helen or Iris. He was obsessed with the need for money and it was an obsession that grew stronger with time. The Hollisses had so much. They must have millions. That house alone was worth a couple million on today's market and they had paid . . . what for it? Fifty or sixty thousand back in the early 1970s before the real estate boom. They were practically giving houses away then. It was always the same old story: the rich get richer and people like him, artists and teachers, get royally screwed. It occurred to him that Holliss was a teacher, but of course he was rich besides. Moreover he was a Stanford professor, one of those privileged bastards who showed up twice a week and blatted out the same old lectures year after year and then complained they were underpaid. He knew that type. Holliss was just exactly that type.

They were crazy for Iris, though, and he was planning to use this to his advantage. He knew she went there almost every day now, having drinks by the pool and taking a nice cool dip, he knew all about it. And he allowed it. "Whatever makes you happy," he had told her. His plan was not fully formed yet, but in general he wanted them to fall even more in love with her, grow dependent on her, and then he would get what he wanted. He was not sure how, but he'd make them pay up. They could settle money on her. A trust fund or something like that. Or provide her college tuition, maybe. It was possible. At least it was not impossible. It would only take a stroke of good luck. He laughed to himself. Another stroke for the old bastard.

IT WAS NOT IMPOSSIBLE at all. Indeed David was the first to bring up the subject. "Shouldn't we do something for that little girl?" he asked. He spoke tentatively as he did everything these days. "She's so bright and she's so lovely, I can't help thinking of Claire as a girl. And shouldn't we be thinking about doing something for her?"

Maggie put down her book. "Well," she said, eager for more.

"Growing up in that family doesn't exactly guarantee a promising future. A warped father, a dissociated mother, God knows what kind of family life."

Maggie interrupted. "Dissociated? You mean catatonic."

"If you prefer. The point I'm making is that Iris is a lovely, intelligent young girl with what could be a fine future, if she makes the right friends, reads the right books"—he paused—"goes to college."

"College is the thing," Maggie said. "We could take care of that. Is that what you're thinking?"

"That's the sort of thing I was thinking."

"Well, that's settled then. The only question is how shall we do it?"

"It's going to take a lot of money."

"We've got a lot of money. We've got your retirement and we still have all that other money." She decided to say it: "Sedgwick money."

"We should have Michael Kelly decide how to do it. He can set it up so that it can be used only by Iris and only for education and then that father of hers can't get his hands on it."

"Shall I call and make an appointment with Kelly?"

"Shouldn't we discuss it first?"

"We've just discussed it and I think you made a number of convincing arguments. Now we should just do it. Do you want me to call Kelly or do you think it should come from you? Men like to talk to the man when it's a question of money. So I think you should call him. Tomorrow. After our walk."

"What do you make of that, Dickens?" David said, and patted him on the head.

Dickens blinked in appreciation.

———

DAVID WAS COMING OUT of himself at last. Maggie saw this as a sign that he had decided to rejoin life, thanks to Iris and her winning innocence. They had not yet phoned Michael Kelly about setting up a trust for Iris's education, but Maggie was determined they would do that soon. Meanwhile they had this wonderful child all to themselves.

Iris visited every day. She and David finished reading *Jane Eyre* and moved on to *Great Expectations*. David did all the voices and Iris was delighted. He was particularly good as Joe Gargery and Mrs. Joe.

"He wanted to be an actor," Maggie said to Iris. She realized after she said it that it was probably true. "Is that right, David?"

"I wanted to act but I never had the courage to try."

"Claire has the courage and apparently she's good. Or at least she was good in that Albee play."

"Anybody would be good in that play. It's a foolproof role for any actress. Failure proof. You know what I mean."

Suddenly Iris spoke up. "My daddy says she's a brilliant actress."

David and Maggie exchanged a look that was not lost on Iris. Maggie said, "Has your daddy ever seen Aunt Claire acting?"

"He hasn't seen her, but he writes about her in his book. It's his new book." She paused. "It's confidential."

"Then we won't ask anything about it," Maggie said.

"I don't mind," Iris said. "I read it all the time on the computer."

"But it's confidential. So we won't ask about it. And you shouldn't talk about it."

Iris blushed and murmured, "I'm sorry," and very soon decided she should go home.

After she left, David turned to Maggie and asked, "What's this about a book with Claire in it?"

"They had a thing, David, but it's all over. It's nothing."

"But he's writing about her? In a book?"

"Apparently."

"And about us?"

"Claire thinks so, but you know how Reginald is. It will never come to anything."

"And what's this about a thing they had? Do you mean an affair? A sexual thing?"

"You know Claire."

"I *knew* Claire. I don't think I know *this* Claire. When the hell did all this happen?"

"Now, don't get all worked up. Think of your health. It's not worth bringing on another stroke."

"Well, tell me. Just fill me in—if you would, please—on what's been going on while I was being a good sport about dying."

"That's it exactly. Being a good sport about dying. That's what they want from a good patient, isn't it. For you to die quietly and be a good sport about it. Not make a fuss. Not inconvenience people. Even that handsome doctor with all the good news."

"Don't change the subject, Maggie."

"All right. All right. As I understand it, Claire had a little fling with Reginald while you were in the hospital, but it came to nothing very soon. She found him a bore, I think, but every-thing's fine now because in some bizarre way he seems devoted to that poor Helen. Thank God for that."

"And they email one another. Reginald said she emailed him about my stroke."

"I suppose they do. Everybody emails. Everybody twitters and tweets and skypes, except us. Anyway it's all over and we can all rest in peace."

They were silent for a while, each of them anxious not to upset the other. Finally the silence was too much for David.

"Go back to this book. This confidential book."

"It's nothing. It's nothing at all. It's one of his Ds of G."

"It better be. A delusion."

"His whole life is a delusion."

"I'll sue the bastard if he writes about us. The goddam nerve!"

"Calm down. You're upsetting Dickens. You're upsetting me as well."

Dickens whimpered beneath the table.

"I am calm. I'm perfectly calm. I'm just saying." He took a deep breath and exhaled slowly. "There," he said. "He's an idiot, isn't he, Dickens. Yes, he is. Yes, he is."

The doorbell rang and it was Iris. She was nervous, near tears. "I want to apologize, Mrs. Holliss, for being indiscreet. I'm sorry." She turned quickly and went down the path. She did not look back.

"Indiscreet!" Maggie said. "How can you not love this girl?" Despite her efforts not to, she burst into tears.

David took her in his arms, determined he would not cry.

"That child will be the death of us," he said.

———————

REGINALD WROTE A lengthy email to Claire in which he set out a scene from his new novel. In the scene the actress Carla Holloway gave a magnificent performance as Hedda Gabler and established herself as the new Meryl Streep. Carla was a short, square woman of unconventional beauty who was famous for her frankness and integrity, personality traits that served her admirably on the stage: thus far the character of Claire. The scene itself was largely narrative, its only drama arising from Reginald's overinsistence on the greatness of her performance. Its primary intention was to win Claire's approval, and of course it succeeded.

Claire read the scene and saw at once what he was doing—anything that would elicit her approval—and she was pleased that he had taken the trouble to repair their relationship, even though his methods were crude and obvious.

"Brava for Carla!" she wrote back. "Very subtly done. Now let me see what you're doing to poor Misery and Poop."

Reginald smiled as he read her email. He wanted her on his side. He needed her approval. It was no longer a question of getting more information on Misery and Poop or the screwed-up sons. No, it was a psychological thing that he recognized in himself: the need for approval of what, in any case, he was determined to do. He would finish them off.

Meanwhile he would go for a midnight walk. He was determined to have the last word.

DICKENS DIED DURING THE NIGHT. He always slept at the door to their bedroom, spread out across the entrance to protect them from whatever dangers lurked in the darkened house. When David woke that morning, Dickens was in his place, his head resting on his paws, his eyes closed, with no thump of his tail in greeting. David realized at once what had happened. He woke Maggie and together they sat on the floor beside the dog. They said nothing for a long while and then David said, "I'll carry him down to the kitchen and we'll call the vet."

"I'll help," Maggie said, but in the end it was easier for David to carry the dead dog by himself.

"He was such a good dog," Maggie said.

"He's better off now," David said. He wiped away a tear. "He's in a better place."

A better place? Maggie wondered what had happened to her husband.

26.

They took their morning walks without Dickens. These were sad walks because Dickens remained very much a presence to them: his sudden bolt in pursuit of a squirrel, his friendly greeting to anyone who stopped to say hello, his doggy sounds of pleasure and surprise and sheer animal joy in being alive. But he was no longer alive and they missed him.

One September morning, cooler after a long hot spell, they met Reginald Parker out walking. They had not seen him in some time and he seemed older, he looked unwell, and he was distinctly unhappy.

"Good morning," he said. "No Dickens, I see."

"No Dickens," David said, surprised by this assault.

"That must be hard for you. The dog's death."

"I'm sure you understand," Maggie said.

"I do. I know all about loss."

Neither Maggie nor David replied.

"Which brings to mind my daughter. Iris has been spending much too much time over there with you and I think that should be stopped."

"We love having her visit," Maggie said. "We love . . ."

"But she's *my* daughter."

"I see," David said. "Yes, she's your daughter."

"Therefore I've told her no more visits."

"I see," David said again.

"It's not healthy for a nine-year-old to be spending her afternoons with old people. She should be out playing with children her own age."

"Of course," Maggie said, and David echoed her, "Of course."

"I hope that's clear."

"It's clear. We'll miss her, of course."

"You should think of her as Dickens. Just another loss. You're looking quite well, by the way, after your stroke, David. Not much damage, I guess."

"Well, we can always hope for more," David said.

There seemed to be nothing further to say. They merely looked at each other expectantly.

"Have a nice day," Reginald said, and he made no effort to conceal his satisfaction. It was a first step. He was not sure what the next would be.

DAVID WAS DETERMINED he would not be defeated by this. Reginald would give in as soon as he needed money and they would get to see Iris again. Besides, Maggie would think of something. Meanwhile he needed a healthy distraction. He needed to write. As soon as he got home he went to his study and piled up his research books on Gissing. He would deal with his rage by immersing it in work, and not the research kind of work any longer but the honest hard work of writing. He sat at the computer dizzy with anger, wondering how anybody managed to write anything. It all seemed impossible. He could see nowhere to begin and so he wrote down some facts. There was no arguing with facts.

George Gissing was born on 22 November 1857 at Thompson's Yard in Wakefield, Yorkshire. His mother was Margaret Bedford and his father was Thomas Walter Gissing, a chemist. He was the first of five children, the others being William, Algernon, Margaret, and Ellen.

In 1872 he placed twelfth in the Oxford local examinations and in 1874 he placed first in England in both Latin and English in his BA exam at the University of London. In 1875 he fell in love with a prostitute, Marianne Harrison, and to help support her he began stealing from his fellow students. He was found out, tried, and sentenced to a month's hard labor at Belle Vue Prison in Manchester. He was expelled from college . . . he was unlucky in love, unlucky in marriage . . . he wrote some twenty-three books in twenty-three years . . . his poverty was a constant . . .

DAVID LOOKED AT THAT for a long moment, wondering if there had ever been a more unpromising start to a literary biography. Probably not. Nonetheless he went on with it and after an hour he found that he had written a terrible hodgepodge of Gissing's life and works, a kind of diary entry, but—astonishingly—he felt he had made a beginning and could at last start to write.

And, he realized, during the time it took to write this, he had put Reginald completely out of his mind.

"I'VE PUT AN END to Iris's visits," Reginald wrote. He intended to keep Claire informed about his relations with her family so that she could bring some pressure on them to help out. It was wrong that they should have all that money when he had barely enough to get by on.

It was true—he could hear their objections—it was true that the money he spent on drugs could go toward paying his bills and putting food on the table, but the poor had to live, too. The poor needed air and light and beauty just as much as the Hollisses. "If you have two pennies, buy bread with one and with the other buy a hyacinth for your soul." Some Persian poet said that and he was right.

He decided to put off telling Claire about his triumph over the Hollisses. Instead he highlighted a long section from his new novel—on the stinginess of David and the selfishness of Maggie—and copied it to the email he'd begun and sent it on, without comment, to Claire. It was just and good and very, very funny. She'd love it.

———————

CLAIRE WAS AT FIRST confused by Reginald's email and then she found herself indignant and finally she was filled with rage. Who did this idiot think he was? "I've put an end to Iris's visits." That was cruel. Maggie and David loved the child and it was the act of a vicious man to deprive two old people of the company of someone they loved just because he had the power to do so. What could possess him? At once, of course, she knew what possessed him: drugs. She had seen druggies and their inspired cruelty in the Oregon commune and she knew that the drug train generally ran nonstop on its way to disaster. "I've put an end to Iris's visits," he wrote. Poor Misery and Poop. Poor Iris.

She read on, amused at first by the idea of a satiric novel about her family. But at once she bristled at the character of Donald. He bore an uncanny physical resemblance to David but the likeness ended there. Donald's stinginess was so overblown that it was ridiculous, incredible; he was a mere caricature with no emotional or intellectual life whatsoever. And yet he was supposed to be a Stanford University professor who had written books on Thackeray and Crane and was the proud father of the actress Carla Holloway and two loser sons, one of them gay and the other impotent. He was one-dimensional, a stick figure. Donald's wife, Molly, was another stick figure. Her single quality was self-centeredness, and her devotion to their ugly dog—poor Dickens, she thought—was the only redeeming aspect of her appalling character. The writing itself was graceful enough. The prose was fluid and for the most part free from the metaphorical posturing she would have expected from Reginald. And no metaphysics at all; only malice and envy. She read straight through to the end. What to make of this? Was he losing it entirely?

Claire printed out the email. She would meditate on it over a cup of tea.

DAVID WAS WORKING FULL time on his book. That meant a quick morning walk with Maggie and then a long slog at the computer. Their walk was silent for the most part, while he turned over in his mind what he would write when he got home, and then he'd make a cup of coffee to place beside his computer and grow cold while he wrote. He found the writing less difficult than ever before and he wondered if this was just a gift of age or a lucky fluke or maybe it meant he was actually going to finish this book before he dropped dead. He had always considered the Gissing biography a project that would never be finished and he was comfortable with that. It was something to talk about, something to think about, something to keep you busy while you waited for death. But now, for the first time, he wanted to finish it. He could see it as a whole, a finished work, an actual accomplishment. He would dedicate it to the women in his life: to Maggie, to Iris.

Suddenly Maggie appeared at the door to his study. It was afternoon and he was still seated at his computer.

"I think you should take a little break," she said, "and discuss what we're going to do about Iris."

"Fine," he said. "I'll be there in a minute."

"Are you all right? You look so vague. Like you've lost it."

"Goddammit, I've been trying to write."

"So shoot me," she said. "Forget about the coffee. I'll have it by myself."

"This is what comes of thinking nice thoughts about difficult people," he said, but Maggie had already left him. He could hear her in the kitchen banging cups and saucers and abusing the coffee maker.

He joined her in the kitchen, guilty although he had no need to be, and he put his arms around her from behind.

"My sweet," he said. "Did I not give you proper attention? Are we feeling neglected? Have I left you for George Gissing?"

"I wouldn't mind Gissing. I never mind when you're working. It's just that, well, I guess it's just that I miss her. Iris, I mean. What can we do?"

"We can have a cup of coffee and talk about it. Now give us a kiss."

She gave him a dutiful kiss and they had their coffee and, after an endless hour of frustration and anxiety, they agreed that they could do nothing. Iris was not their child. Alas. Iris would never be their child.

"I THINK YOU'RE VERY SICK," Claire said.

She had violated their rules by calling him on the phone. Reginald was pleased.

"It's nice to speak to you, too."

"It's one thing to write satire, it's another to commit libel."

"They can't prove libel. Everything I wrote is true."

"It's slander."

"Which is it, libel or slander?"

"It's bad writing, to be frank."

Reginald was silent at that.

"You know I'm always frank. I always tell the truth."

"It's not bad writing. It's . . ."

"It's druggie writing." She waited. "I can hear the drugs in the prose."

"Only weed. And sometimes coke."

"Are you on the hard stuff? I think you must be on the hard stuff."

"And if I was? If I were?"

"If you were, I'd say come off it. If you weren't, I'd say you've lost perspective on what makes a character real. Read Chekhov. Read Ibsen. Read Kaufman and Hart, for God's sake. Nobody is simply bad. He has to have some redeeming qualities or we won't believe him. Your Donald character isn't even funny. He's just a product of your anger. Nobody is that simple."

Reginald hung up the phone but Claire continued on.

"Besides," she said, "it's one thing for me to tell you about old Poop being stingy and another for you to make him ridiculous. Family always talk about family, and it's okay for them but not for outsiders. You don't get to do this. You just don't."

She listened for a response and heard only the dial tone. But she was not done yet.

"I think you're very sick," she said, satisfied for the moment.

After another cup of tea she phoned Reginald again and when he answered, she said merely, "I'm going to tell my father on you," and hung up.

HELEN HAD FINALLY WORKED up her courage to ask her boss for full-time work off the books and offered to split the extra money with him. He asked her many questions about how this would play out, who would get what percentage of money, and how they would manage to keep the deal quiet. Their discussion went on for some time. In the end he told her that what she proposed was not only illegal but immoral and so he would have to let her go. But she was a good worker, he said, and she would only be laid off rather than fired, so at some future date she could be hired by Walmart again.

She reported this to Reginald, who was certain she had mishandled the proposition but he did his best to conceal his anger. The result was she'd be home all the time now until she found another job and they'd have no income at all and he was off drugs for good.

Christ, was there no end to the misery?

27

Reginald could not concentrate on his writing and he felt guilty for sleeping late and, now that she was unemployed, he found Helen very annoying. She did not seem to know what to do with herself and she was always in the way. She went through the Help Wanted columns every morning before he was up, making lists of jobs and phone numbers, but she was hopelessly unqualified for anything good, and the other jobs—the possible ones—were already taken by the time she phoned about them.

"Isn't there something I can do to help you?" she asked.

Reginald thought, *Yes, go away,* but instead he said, "Writing is a completely solitary job, you know that."

"But I could type or something."

"I just need quiet."

"I won't say a word. I'll just sit here and read."

She read for a while and then said, "Can I make you some coffee?"

"I'm trying to concentrate." He had been sitting in front of his computer for the past twenty minutes, unable to think of anything to write, in fact unable to think of anything except Helen, exasperatingly quiet, in the same room with him. It was bad enough that she had no job and brought no money home, but it was unendurable to have her sitting here, waiting to be helpful.

"I've got to go for a walk," he said.

"Do you want me to come with you?" she asked.

"I've got to think," he said.

"I could be quiet and just be with you."

"I've got to think," he said again.

It came to him then that he would make one last appeal to the Hollisses. He would ring their doorbell and confront them and insist they make him a loan. He would explain his situation. He was a good man and a good father. He was a writer. He needed money not just for himself and not for Helen. But for Iris.

CLAIRE HAD DELAYED TELLING her parents the kind of thing Reginald was writing about them and their sons because she was a little embarrassed at getting off so lightly herself. Still, she thought they should know, not so much because he would make fools of them in public but because she intuited from Reginald's anger that something was very wrong with him. She had seen his kind in the commune and she guessed that, fueled with drugs, he could turn violent with the least provocation. And it was very clear to her that he had it in for David. Poor old Poop, who wouldn't hurt a flea.

She could only guess how Maggie and David were getting along without Iris. They had all but adopted the child and now she was cut off from them . . . like their own children. Reginald had a streak of cruelty in him, no doubt about it. She thought about that. Even when he made love, he would hold himself back, depriving her of that deeper pleasure she had earned. And deserved. In justice.

She decided that Misery and Poop should be alerted to Reginald's satire and so she sat down and wrote them a quick email.

Dear Old Things:

I hope you're coming along well, Daddy, and I hope Mother is being nice to you. I can only imagine how hard it is for you both without Dickens. I see him in my mind's eye walking between you each morning and taking off after squirrels and enjoying his naps under the kitchen table. I'm sure you miss him a lot.

I'm writing to tell you about Reginald's new project. You ought to know about it because it's about you. That is, you're the subject—maybe the object—of his satiric novel about academics. There's no need to worry because it will never be published, but I think you should know he's doing it. I'll attach the part of the manuscript he sent me and you can see what he's up to. Up to no good, because it's so one-sided and hateful. But better you should know.

I'm playing Miss Preen in *The Man Who Came to Dinner*. She is the nurse to Sheridan Whiteside, the main character. She walks out on him to take a job in a munitions factory, she says, to help in the destruction of the human race. It's a role I understand well and I intend to make it a big hit.

This was the friendliest note she'd written them in years, and she reflected that it was easier to be nice to them when they weren't around than when they were. This was true of her son, too, poor unimaginative Gaius, and—now that she thought of it—it was true of Willow as well. People were nicer at a distance; the further away they were, the nicer they seemed. It struck her that she had begun to identify with Nurse Preen. She was sinking into the role, hating the human race. This was the stuff of great acting.

She sat back from her computer, breathless once more at the idea of being the real thing. Then she highlighted the file Reginald had sent her and attached it to her email and signed it, "Love you, Claire." She thought about that for a moment and changed Claire to Chiara and, with a congratulatory smile, she pressed Send. "There it is, a love note to Misery and Poop."

REGINALD RANG THE HOLLISSES' doorbell and waited. He was nervous, of course, but determined. And he had fortified himself with a thin line of coke. He pressed the bell and waited. It was ten in the morning. Surely they were home.

Though Maggie always opened the door to anyone who rang, for some reason this morning she looked through the peephole and was appalled to see Reginald, looking furious, on her doorstep. She put her hand on the doorknob and was about to open the door when the thought crossed her mind that no good could come of this. She stood there, frozen.

Reginald rang the doorbell again and waited. He would stand his ground. He would wait them out.

Maggie stood, silent, on the other side of the door.

Reginald opened the screen door and put his hand on the doorknob. He could not bring himself to turn it. What if the door was unlocked? What if it opened?

Inside, Maggie heard the screen door open. What if he tried the door? She looked down and saw that it was unlocked. They never locked the door during the day. She blushed, embarrassed. But why should *she* be embarrassed? She was determined suddenly to keep him out. She leaned hard against the door.

Reginald turned the doorknob and felt the door move inward slightly. He pulled his hand away as if the knob were on fire. So they were home, the selfish bastards, and would not open to him.

Maggie closed her eyes and waited.

Reginald, angry and confused, gave up and went away. Maggie leaned against the door exhausted.

A minute later David came out of his study and said, "Someone's at the door."

"It's nobody," Maggie said.

It wasn't until lunchtime that she calmed down enough to tell him what had happened.

"Incredible!" David said. "We should remember to lock the door from now on, even during the day."

"What are we coming to in this world?" Maggie said.

"The end, eventually," David said and went back to his study to continue writing about Gissing: the early, miserable years.

———

MAGGIE AND DAVID SHARED the same email address and, since David was occupied with Gissing, Maggie got to read Claire's email first. She wondered if she could erase it somehow before David saw it and had another stroke, but she knew that erasing was futile because everything got through to him anyhow. And she knew he would eventually have to face the fact that Reginald was writing about them. A satiric novel, no less. In the abstract it was just a silly idea but this email was not abstract. David/Donald was a monster of selfishness and she was simply a self-centered idiot who doted on her dog. Poor Dickens. Why did Dickens have to be dragged into it? But at least Dickens was safely dead. It was David she worried about.

She waited until he came out of his study, tired, blinking a little, as if he were emerging from a cave.

"How did it go?" she said, but before he could respond she told him everything: Claire was in *The Man Who Came to Dinner*, playing a nurse who hated the human race, and—by the way—Reginald was writing a nasty book in which they were featured players. Characters. He was actually putting words on paper. He had already put them on paper or at least on the computer screen. It was on Claire's email—a selection from the novel—and he shouldn't get upset because it was ridiculous. It was simply ridiculous. Ridiculous! Maybe he should wait to read it until he calmed down.

David said he was as calm as he was ever going to be and

went to his study to read Claire's email. He came back, pale, defeated, a half hour later.

"It's ridiculous," he said. "You're right."

Maggie didn't know what to make of this. She had expected rage.

"Moreover he's a terrible writer." He thought for a moment. "Do you think he wants to extort money with this thing?"

"I have a confession," she said. "When he returned the second loan, the four hundred dollars, he was short by two hundred." She could tell that David did not understand. "I should have told you at the time."

"What are you talking about?"

"Lies make everything wrong," she said. "Let's just ignore him."

And so they talked for an hour and had some nice hot tea and talked for another hour and finally decided to ignore Reginald's novel and Reginald himself. It was a decision they arrived at easily. Living with it would be another thing. And living without Iris.

HELEN FELT HELPLESS. Unable to find a new job and caught up in her husband's desperation, she had left innumerable handwritten notes at neighborhood doors offering to clean house, care for pets, run errands, et cetera, but of course everyone in Professorville already had cleaners and pet carers and errand runners. There was no response to her notes. And she had nobody to turn to. She thought of approaching the Hollisses to ask for help but she realized that Reginald would regard this as interfering in his life and she would never dare do that.

He was a changed man. The drugs were making him distant, hostile, and she had begun to fear him. He was no longer writing and he ate almost nothing. He was silent most of the time and when he spoke to her at all, it was with a kind of resentment. She had to find a job. She had to get him some money.

Suddenly, for no reason she could think of, she was tempted to read his book. Back when he had worked on it regularly—weeks ago—he had printed out each day's work and put it in a folder beneath a pile of books on the floor next to his computer desk. It was understood that his writing must never be touched, but just to be safe he piled the books on top as a kind of deterrent. She had been offended when he first did this, since surely he knew she would never violate his privacy. But now that he was drifting from her into a terrifying world she recognized as craziness, she reached out to his writing as some kind of contact with the old Reginald, the loving man she married.

She moved the books carefully, in a single pile, so she could put them back exactly as they had been and he'd never know what she had done. She opened the folder and took the first page in her hand. It was the title page: *What Is Not Being Said.* The next was the dedication page: To Helen. Tears came to her eyes. She was tempted to go on to the novel itself but seeing the dedication so surprised and upset her that she closed the folder at once and returned it to its place on the floor beside the desk. She positioned the little pile of books exactly as it had been. Two minutes later, though, consumed by curiosity about this wonderful manuscript, she returned to the folder and began reading.

MEANWHILE REGINALD RANG the Hollisses' doorbell again and waited. It was a beautiful warm October afternoon, a Saturday, and he had Iris by his side. Surely they would open to her. She had begged not to come but he insisted. She could do at least this much for the family, he said.

A hard week had passed since his last attempt on the Hollisses and Reginald was looking worse each day. He had been taking his long nightly walks to East Palo Alto and sleeping late in the morning and subsisting for the most part on coffee and marijuana since the coke was all gone.

He stood beside Iris and rang the bell once more. They had been standing there for what seemed an hour. He checked his watch. Three minutes had passed.

He opened the screen and knocked on the inside door. He knocked a second time and then he tried the doorknob. It turned and, with a slight pressure, he pushed the door open. He stepped inside, holding Iris by the hand.

"We shouldn't," Iris said.

They moved from the foyer to the living room, where they could look out into the back garden and see Maggie and David reclining on lounge chairs looking out over the pool.

So they hadn't heard the bell after all. A good sign.

"Please, no," Iris said softly.

Reginald, still holding Iris's hand, moved through the living room to the kitchen and out the back door to the patio. The door slammed behind them and David turned to see what was happening. Maggie sat forward in her chair.

"What's this?" David said, but it was not a question. He looked at Reginald in disbelief. The man looked years older, his beard was graying and straggly, he was bent over holding Iris's hand. He could be sixty. And David could scarcely recognize Iris.

Reginald suddenly found himself with nothing to say. He stood there beside the pool looking at them. The Hollisses. His salvation.

"You've got to help me," he said.

"How did you get in here?" David asked.

"You've got to help."

"How did you get in?" His voice was angry, indignant.

"The door was unlocked. We rang the bell."

David looked at Maggie and said nothing. She had forgotten to lock the door.

"There's no money. There's no food. There's nothing. You've got to loan me a thousand dollars."

"We made our last loan a couple months ago. I told you, no more loans."

Iris, who had been standing next to her father with her eyes cast down, now looked up at David and then at Maggie. She flushed red.

"Nine hundred then. I need food for my family."

David looked at Maggie and saw no sign of what he ought to do. They had reached a terrible moment and their lives depended on his doing what was right. The money had ceased to be the issue. What mattered now was principle.

"I'm sorry," David said.

"I'm begging you."

"Please go before you make this worse than it is already."

Suddenly Reginald lost control. Tears poured down his face and he began to babble. "You have everything and we have nothing. You call yourself Christians and you've never heard of being your brother's keeper. You keep it all for yourself. It's a crime against justice. Claire knows what you are. Please, please, for my wife and daughter, please loan me money. You're the last place I can turn to."

"Leave now or I'll call the police," David said.

Maggie put her hands over her face.

"Tell them, Iris!" Reginald said. "Ask them for money!"

"I'm sorry," Iris said.

"How can you betray me like this? Ask them! Tell them!"

"I'm sorry." She began to cry.

Speechless now, Reginald put his hands on Iris's shoulders and shook her. It was an automatic gesture. He did not seem to know what he was doing.

"Stop!" David shouted. "Stop that! I'll give you the money."

Reginald shook her again, then he released her and patted her shoulders.

"I'll give you the damned money," David said.

Reginald stared at them and at the swimming pool beyond them and then, for just a moment, he came to himself. He looked around as if he were awakening from a nightmare.

"I wouldn't touch your money now," he said. "You can give it to Iris. She's all you care about anyway."

He wiped the tears from his face, pulled himself together, and left them. As he went through the kitchen he tipped over the cookie jar and heard it shatter on the floor. He did not look back. He was done with them. He slammed the door behind him.

28.

Maggie and David tried to hold themselves together until Iris left, difficult as that was. "I wouldn't touch your money now," Reginald had said. And he stormed through the kitchen and out the front door.

Iris stood there in tears until Maggie folded her in her arms and let her cry herself out. That took a long time. David sat back in his lounge chair and concentrated on not having a stroke. When he was at last able to speak, he said, "It's all right, sweetheart, everything will be all right."

He got up then with some difficulty—he was dizzy and he kept tilting to the left—and went inside and wrote Reginald a check for a thousand dollars. He put it in an envelope and brought it outside. Maggie was stretched out on the lounge chair now with Iris in her arms.

"Give this to your father, Iris, and tell him it's not a loan. It's a gift." He put his hand on her head, a kind of paternal blessing, and said, "We'll always love you. You know that, don't you."

"You should go now," Maggie said. "Your father will be worried. And your mother."

Iris left and David poured each of them a stiff shot of brandy.

He poured a second one for himself. They remained silent. This was not the time for a discussion.

REGINALD HAD SAID he was done with them but he knew he was not. He wanted more than money; he wanted vengeance for this latest humiliation. To be reduced to begging! And in front of his own daughter! It was too much. And Iris herself had betrayed him. She was old enough and, God knows, smart enough to understand exactly what she was doing. Telling them she was sorry. Apologizing for her father's tears, for his begging. Well, they would pay for this. And pay.

Helen was not at the door to greet him. She was seated on the couch, a woman of leisure, reading. For her intellectual improvement, he had no doubt. And then he realized—but it couldn't be possible—that she was reading the manuscript of his novel. His vision clouded for a moment and the room went red and then black, and then he came back to himself. She was reading his book. Something inside him twisted against his heart and he thought, *This is death. This is what it means to die.* He felt rage rise in his throat. He swallowed, hard, and said, "Well?"

Helen only looked at him. She was very sad.

"Well?" he said again, frightened now.

"I thought better of you," she said. "I thought you were a good man."

"I should kill you," he said. "I should obliterate you from the face of the earth." His heart was pumping wildly and he felt he was about to do something he would regret forever, so he turned to leave her.

At that moment Iris came through the door. Reginald whirled on her as if he were being attacked and said, "You!"

Iris handed him the envelope and, looking down, said, "They said it's a gift. It's not a loan."

He took the envelope and tore it in half. He threw the two halves in Helen's direction and watched while they fluttered to the carpet. He turned then and slammed out of the house.

They were all traitors. All of them.

IT WAS LONG PAST midnight when Reginald returned from his walk to East Palo Alto. He had met up with his longtime supplier and they had done some crystal meth. He had been able to push back the feelings of betrayal for several hours and he was calm now and thinking clearly. He knew how to get back at all of them, economically, with one sharp blow.

Helen was asleep, the bottle of Ambien still open on the bathroom sink. He took two of the pills and filled a glass with water and went into Iris's room. She was lying awake, staring into the dark.

"Daddy," she said. "I'm sorry." She pointed to the envelope beside her bed. She had taped the two halves of the check together.

"It's all right," Reginald said. "Everything is going to be all right. Just take these two pills and you'll get a nice sleep and when you wake up everything will be just the way you've always wanted it."

She took the two pills.

"I'm sorry," she said again.

"Shhh," he said. "Try to sleep. I'll sit by you until you drift off."

It was not long before she fell into a deep sleep. He waited another half hour, telling himself to be calm, be resolute. This would not be easy.

He lifted Iris out of her bed and, because it was a chilly night, he wrapped her in her pink blanket. He carried her to the door, which he held open with one foot, and sidled through it and out into the dim moonlight. There was a tiny sliver of moon and only a few stars as he made his way through the dark street. This was a night world he was familiar with. It existed in a half-light at the edge of his consciousness. He could hear the suppressed anger in the houses he passed, he knew the sounds they made telling lies in their sleep, not one of them walking in the way of the Lord. He could pull down a curse on every one of them, liars and hypocrites as they were.

He cradled Iris's sleeping body against his chest.

He turned left at the end of the street and approached the Hollisses' house. There were no lights on, of course. This had been an ordinary day for them: humiliating a neighbor, crushing another human being, and then writing a check to be rid of any problem of conscience. A thousand dollars. A cheap way out. They loved Iris. They had won her away from him.

He let himself into their back garden by the side gate. It was supposed to be kept locked as an insurance measure against some neighbor kid getting injured at their pool, but they never remembered to lock it. They would remember now.

He went to the edge of the pool and paused while he looked for the best place to begin. There were a few steps leading down into the deep end of the pool and he chose these. He dropped the pink blanket by the side of the pool and walked down the steps until the water reached his knees. Gently he lowered Iris, facedown, into the water. She stirred, but he was ready for her. With one hand beneath her chest and the other on the back of her head, he pushed her face beneath the water and held her there. A stream of bubbles disturbed the water and suddenly she was fully alive, struggling wildly against his hands, but he was too strong for her and, though she thrashed the water and at one point managed to cry out, he held her beneath the surface until at last she stopped struggling and went quiet. He continued to hold her underwater while he recited the Our Father. It was a good death, a quiet death.

He was exhausted. He got out of the water and stretched out beside the pool. Iris's body sank, which surprised him, until he realized it would be some little time before she would float— she would be found floating—safe at last from their love. And from his.

He was calm. He had done what he had to do. It remained now only to go home and destroy his novel, erase it from his computer, and wait for the police. He had always made fun of *CSI* and

PART FIVE

❖ ❖ ❖

n the final months of 2010 the lone terrorist—passionate, reckless—had emerged as the new enemy in the battle against reason. Forget Iraq, forget Afghanistan. The FBI, the CIA, and the Pentagon focused their intense concentration on an unidentifiable enemy, the committed killer who acted alone. He could be anyone. He could be your neighbor. Just check the daily headlines.

Iris's death and her father's confession of guilt were front-page news in the local papers, but national interest in the case was almost immediately displaced by yet another mass shooting at a high school in Arizona. One drowned little girl had no chance against twelve teenagers gunned down by a classmate they had bullied. The local papers, however, held on. Her own father had drowned her! What were we coming to? How could this happen in a civilized community? Was it drugs or insanity or some sexual kink? Blame the Hollisses, the father said! Reporters were at the Hollisses' door every day, demanding an interview, lurking behind shrubbery, sneaking in back to photograph the swimming pool where the child had been drowned. Eventually the reporters would go, but meanwhile Maggie and David sealed themselves in their house and waited.

Maggie, stunned and broken, pulled herself together long enough to phone the children and tell them not to worry: she and David were surviving the awful attention, Iris was a ghastly loss to them, but above all do not come home. The less attention, the better. Claire insisted on coming west to see them, but Maggie held firm. Repeat: do not come home.

They were like people who had survived some terrible plane crash and were not convinced they were still alive. They were staggered by grief and overwhelmed by guilt. For several days they did not talk about their part in Iris's death; they did not talk at all. Separately however—each very alone—they tortured themselves with possibilities. How much were they to blame? Had they kidnapped the child emotionally? Seduced her away from her family? With money, as Reginald claimed? Had they been right to refuse him money? Money! Always the damned money! Why hadn't they just handed over the thousand dollars? They gave that much to the Pet Rescue Fund every year and never gave it a second thought, so why not give it to Reginald instead? If only for Iris's sake. Why?

Once they were finally able to talk, they asked each other these questions and answered them and asked them again, always with the shivering fear that they had acted against conscience.

David lay awake at night arguing with himself and found he lost every argument. Maggie lay awake beside him, waiting, afraid the worst would happen.

"If you don't get some rest," she said one night, "you're going to have another stroke."

"Was it my fault?"

"Don't talk nonsense." She was loyal still. "You did what you thought was the right thing. It was the goddam money we should blame."

And on the following night: "It *was* the right thing. Wasn't it? To refuse him?"

"Was it?

"Wasn't it? I thought . . ."

"Who ever knows for certain what the right thing is!"

"But we talked about it . . . we agreed . . . we both . . ."

She lay there, silent, sullen, and then she relented. "Reginald is a sick man," she said.

And on another night: "So you think I was wrong to refuse him money?"

"You're *not* to blame." She was lying for his sake. "We're not to blame."

"I wish I could be certain."

"You're going to bring on a stroke, David."

"I know. God's justice . . . if there was a God."

She was alarmed by his mention of God and not for the first time. What next? A stroke, at the least.

THE STROKE, when it came, seemed mild at first. No pain, just a dull throbbing in the right carotid artery. Too much worry. Too little exercise. They had been under journalistic house arrest for too long and they were both a little crazy. What they needed was a good walk and fresh air.

Then David discovered he could not walk at all, could not even get up from his chair. And the left side of his face was rigid. *This one*, he said to himself, *is a full-on stroke*. He tried to say this to Maggie, but what came out was an indecipherable growl. Maggie choked back her tears and called 911.

David was hospitalized at once.

THIS TIME, Maggie told herself, she would not make the mistake of telling the children about the stroke. She stayed by David's bedside until there was good news—the clot had not burst, the paralysis would pass—and she put off the chaos and injured feelings of another family visit until some date far in the future . . . perhaps when she herself was dead.

One morning sitting by his bed, nodding in and out of a kind of sleep, she thought about how much trouble money had caused in their lives. David's resentment of the Sedgwick money, Reginald's murderous demands for money, her own children's endless need to borrow money against their inheritance.

Money. Always money.

It came to her as a kind of revelation: she should get rid of it. The children wanted it. Let them have it. It was that simple.

A feeling of great relief came over her, she felt free, she felt clean.

She saw her lawyer that afternoon and laid out her plans. A third to each of them, minus their early withdrawals, and with one signature the Sedgwick money would be gone. She and David could live on Social Security and his TIAA-CREF pension and that would be that.

The lawyer was astonished and cautioned her against making decisions in haste, especially when David was ill and couldn't rightly assist her in disposing of so much money, and did she realize she was talking about stocks worth in excess of three million?

"It's my money," she said, "it's Sedgwick money, and I intend to get rid of it. Now. For good."

"That's your right," he said grudgingly.

"Damned right," she said. "It's mine, and now it's gone."

She left all the little details to the lawyer.

DAVID LAY, SLEEPLESS, in his hospital bed reciting Dickinson poems he had memorized as a boy. *After great pain a formal feeling comes, the nerves sit ceremonious like tombs.* Indeed. Death was on his mind in a way it had never been before. It was tangible. Its taste was bitter. Moreover they had moved him into a room with another patient and he was constantly assaulted by his roommate's labored breathing. It was a constant reminder that death was only one deep breath away.

"You awake?" the roommate said.

"Wide awake," David said. His speech was muddy and he had to speak slowly to make himself understood.

"Can I ask you something?" the roommate said. When there was no reply, he went on, "What do you think of dying?"

"I try not to think of it," David said.

"But when you do. I'm dying and I'm afraid. Pancreatic cancer."

"I'm sorry."

"I'm fifty-six." He breathed in and out several times. "But I trust in God."

David thought, *More fool you*, but he said merely, "I hope that's a consolation."

"I trust in God, don't you? He'll see me through. What do you suppose there is after?"

"After?"

"Do you think there's a heaven and a hell?"

"Schopenhauer called death that long sleep in which individuality is forgotten. I like to think of it that way."

"What way?"

"Aren't you sleepy yet?"

"I'm a born-again Christian. I've accepted Christ as my personal savior."

"And has he accepted you?"

"Oh, yes. He accepts anybody. He'd accept you."

"That's nice. That's very generous of him. You know, I think we should try to get some sleep."

"Sleep in Christ." The man rolled over and sighed. "I have my faith."

David fell asleep almost at once. He dreamed he was back home lying in the sun. The sunlight struck the pool and dazzled his eyes until he thought he saw something purple floating on the surface. There was a sudden clutch at his heart and he knew what would happen next. It was always the same. He leaned forward and shaded his eyes to see more clearly. It was a body. It was Iris.

A scream rose in his throat and he made a choking sound and sat straight up in bed. He had dreamed this dream almost every night since the stroke. He was shaking and covered in sweat.

He woke to the sound of nothing. The usual noises had suddenly ceased—the rubber heels on the tile floors, the squeak of hospital machinery being moved, the low groans and soft whimpers of the hopeful sick. The sudden silence descended on him like a black cloak, it enveloped him and cut off his breath, and he was filled with the terror of dying.

"Don't worry," his roommate whispered. "You'll be all right."

David began to shiver. To calm himself he took a deep breath, but somehow he could not pull the air into his lungs. He began to sweat and his hands began to tremble. He sat up in bed. This would pass in a minute or two. He pressed his knees together and hugged himself. He needed a breath. Only one deep breath. He gulped and flailed. He was suffocating. He was dying. And then it came to him that this is what they meant by a panic attack.

He fought to be calm. He waited a moment and then he gasped for air but still his lungs would not work. He couldn't draw a deep breath and yet, undeniably, he was breathing. But not the way he wanted to, needed to. He tried consciously to inflate his lungs and the air came in but not deep enough. There was a threshold he could not surmount. The light around him grew thinner, darker. His vision was clouded. He inhaled quickly, desperate for just one deep breath, but it eluded him, he could not breathe and he could not breathe and he could not breathe. He let out a low howl of despair. He fell back against the pillows, gasping, and then went unconscious.

When he woke, he was calm again, and breathing.

"You're all right," his roommate said. "It's very scary, dying. You've got to get used to it gradually. It took me nearly a year."

David was silent, humiliated. He had never been afraid of death. It was after all just a return to the nothingness from which we came in the first place. Peace and quiet forever. But it was not peace and quiet that had terrified him. It was nothing: being nothing, thinking nothing, feeling nothing. He was just a dot. A speck. An amoeba. And he did not matter.

"You're lucky to have your faith," he said into the dark, and in that same moment he decided he would never be tempted to belief. At least not from fear.

MAGGIE HIRED A CONSTRUCTION company that tore out the pool and a landscaper who overnight created in its place an autumn garden, complete with mature rosebushes in late bloom. She had not consulted David on getting rid of the Sedgwick money and she did not consult him on getting rid of the pool. What mattered was that nothing be there to remind him of Iris, of her life or her death. It crossed her mind that she was acting like God, powerful and arbitrary, but she said no, she was simply acting as head of the family and she was doing it for love of David. If he lived. If he returned to her alive in body and mind. She looked around at what she had created, the grassy plot, the roses, the air of peace. No more drowning pool, no more self-inflicted nightmare.

It was just another lovely garden, beautiful and empty.

DAVID WAS IN THERAPY for two weeks and then he was sent home to recuperate. His brain was fine, more or less, and his speech was not badly affected, but his hands shook and he was unable to type. He had asked the handsome neurologist if the shaking would get better and he replied that maybe it would, maybe not: "Keep a happy heart," he said, "and pray to God." So that put an end to work on Gissing, David figured. He could now dodder on into senility without the guilt accompanying an unfinished book. He burned his research notes with only a small sense of melodrama and he quite calmly dumped the finished pages of his manuscript into the recycling bin. Sayonara, book.

He liked to lie stretched out in the sun, gazing at the last of the late roses, yellow, salmon, cream colored, and white. He never mentioned the pool nor did he comment on the new garden. It was beautiful and comforting like Maggie herself and he was so humbly grateful he did not know himself. She had created a garden for him so that he could forget. There was no sign left of a pool or a drowning or a little girl in a purple bathing suit. For David, however, Iris was still there. And everlastingly dead.

30

When Maggie finally told him about the Sedgwick money, David merely laughed and shook his head. We'll live on love, he said, like teenagers in a storybook. No, Maggie said, we'll live on love and our retirement money, and if we run short, we'll borrow from our well-set-up children.

It took more than a month for the lawyer to transfer the stocks and notify the children that they were now rich. Each of them responded at once and in his or her own particular way.

Will was the first to write because by sheer chance he got the news before the others. He wrote longhand and sent his thank-you by Royal Mail.

Dear Mother and Father,

Burdened from the start with the yoke of Perfect Son, I was denied the freedom—so generously extended to Sedge and Claire—to explore the possibilities of a lifestyle free of the constraints of familial expectation; i.e., to exercise the nature and limits of my sexual drive (Sedge), to entertain a life lived outside social and academic conventions (Claire), or—and this is as much a problem of our time as it is of you in particular—to experiment with the comforts and solace of a religious faith. I actually tried to be the perfect son. I earned my PhD, I married young, in fact too young, and I fathered three daughters. I did all this for you.

I am so happy to thank you for compensating me now—in this practical way—for all I missed while trying to accommodate your expectations. I feel extraordinarily blessed in my parents and in my marriage. Since news of your gift, Daphne has taken me back into the house and we have great plans for it. We are adding two new bathrooms and a guest room in case you come to visit. We are fixing up the attic room over the garage. The kitchen, already in progress, is going to be a model of British efficiency.

I cannot guess what prompts this sudden and overwhelming generosity, though I imagine it is connected to the tragic death of little Iris, but whatever the reason for it, I thank you and Daphne thanks you and of course our three girls will be eternally grateful.

On the matter of spiritual solace, I hope you will be pleased to learn that Daphne and I are planning to renew our marriage vows in our local Catholic (to you, Anglican) church and we have discussed the possibility of trying for another child, a boy this time perchance.

I have put aside my work on Yeats. I think that by its nature (runes, alas) its appeal was to a limited audience. I have decided instead to write a novel. The working title is The Perfect Son and I leave it to you two

wonderful parents to prognosticate on how it will
unfold.

Daph and I are taking our Christmas holiday in Spain.
Your generous gift has made a great and gracious difference
to our lives.

Your loving, imperfect son, Will

Claire and Sedge responded with emails. Claire's was brief in the extreme:

Fabulous news! I'll fly out to California next week to thank you. Love from your Chiara.

Sedge went on at slightly more length:

Dear Mom and Dad,
    You've outdone yourselves in generosity. Cloris
was saying yesterday that we spend too much money, but I
assured her there's always plenty of money and, sure
enough, now there is. I hope this great gift wasn't made in
haste and I want you to know that if you ever run short, I'm
always here with money to spare and glad to help out.
Cloris is, as she likes to say, over the moon now that she is
pregnant and we are rich. This new marriage and this new
money seem likely to last more than two years.
    With love, Sedge

Maggie responded at once. To Will she wrote: Enjoy the money. We look forward to having The Perfect Son in hand. Love, Mother and Father

To Claire she wrote: Cancel your flight, Chiara mia. We plan to be in Mexico for the next few weeks. See you at Christmas? Love, Misery and Poop

To Sedge she wrote: No need for us to borrow from you yet. Hope everything lasts more than two years. Love, Mom and Dad

With that taken care of, Maggie urged David to go out in the sun while she looked over the accounts. Life was simpler now without the Sedgwick fortune. The bills came in and she paid them and, as Sedge piously believed, there was always plenty of money. Or at least enough. Thus far. She quite liked being comfortably poor.

t was a warm November day, sunny, with no warning that winter was about to descend on them. David was stretched out in his lounge chair by the new rose garden, doing his speech therapy by reciting favorite poems of Frost and Stevens and Emily Dickinson. "After great pain a formal feeling comes" and suddenly Maggie appeared beside him. "'The nerves sit ceremonious like tombs,'" she said. "It's my favorite Dickinson. I brought you a sweater. It's getting a little chilly."

"You're too good to me." He took the sweater in his shaking hands and leaned forward to toss it around his shoulders.

"Would you like some coffee?"

"Just sit with me."

Maggie pulled her lounge chair next to his. They had entered a new relationship of easy dependence and open affection. And there was something more to it, something mystifying, they could not name.

"It's strange sitting here and knowing she's gone."

"It's sad." She waited. "But we have to go on. Everybody does."

A tear came to his right eye, the weak one, and he wiped it away.

She looked at him, an old man now, shattered. And she was left, alive and brittle still.

There was no telling what surprises life held for you. Here was Claire, the mutt of the family, a successful actress in her forties. Sedge and Cloris were married and blissful in their first year, with Cloris pregnant. Perhaps a baby would make the difference and lift the two-year marriage curse from poor Sedge. And Will was back with Daphne, bitterly happy in Essex while she renovated the house and he tortured his academic language into the shape of a novel. And Dickens gone. And Iris gone. And Helen? Nobody knew. She had just disappeared from their lives as silently as she had entered. Poor Helen.

But she and David were still here and she was not done yet.

"I'm going for a walk," she said, "and you're coming with me."

"Oh, I think not."

"I think yes. I'm not done with living, as it's called, and you aren't either. I'm not going to let you." She waited. "And I'm all you've got." She shifted her body closer to him and laid her head on his shoulder.

"My sweetheart," she whispered. "How are you? In yourself."

"Terrified," he said. "But I have you."

She gave him a soft kiss on the ear. Something was happening. Their known lives were slipping away from them.

"I've been thinking," he said.

"I know," she said.

"I've been thinking of God."

"It's not just the stroke?"

"No. I don't think so."

"No," she said.

He went for a moment into one of his silences. "I think if there is a God, he must be you." He shook a little. "Or the image of you."

He wanted to tell her the truth: that in the dark of one long night he had opened himself to the possibility of God and, like a great flood, love had come rushing in. Not love of God but love for her. And with it had come the conviction that all he would ever know of God was this love for her. It overwhelmed all doubt, it justified all hope, it was his beginning and his end.

"Or you're the image of him."

"Discovering God in your old age. And he's me! What a sweetie!" She laughed softly and brushed away a solitary tear.

"I believe in you."

She drew him up from his chair.

"Come on," she said. "Enough malingering. Rise up and walk."

He took a deep breath and looked around him. It was a lovely November afternoon, with no sign of chill to follow. They were alive and lucky to be alive.

"God, what a day!" he said.

"It's almost enough to give a body hope," she said.

EDITOR'S NOTE

The spring semester of my junior year at Stanford, I had one class slot left to fill toward my English major requirement. At that time in my academic career I had taken enough of the department's more arcane courses that I was eager to find one that offered a broader and somewhat less idiosyncratic view toward its particular subject. By chance I encountered one of my dorm mates in White Plaza, and as she was also an English major, I asked if she had any recommendations. "You *have* to take John L'Heureux's class," she answered without hesitation, and told me he was teaching a small seminar on the short story. When I began to explain that it wasn't a subject to which I was especially drawn, she stopped me with a glare and said, "He's the best teacher on campus. Go!"

I went, and if any one decision has been largely responsible for who I am today, it was stepping into John's classroom in the Main Quad. For the next ten weeks I learned how to read astutely and critically (a skill for which high school had left me ill prepared), and, though I didn't realize it at the time, the groundwork was being laid for my future. Over the decades I've met many of John's former students, and have discovered we're all bound by the same affection, respect, and delight at our good fortune to have had him not just as a gifted teacher but as a wise and perceptive mentor. As our own group of a dozen or so sat around a conference table in a classroom in the Old Quad, the spring breezes relieving the room's mustiness with the scent of citrus blossoms from the small grove outside its windows, John entertained, cajoled, demanded, challenged, advocated for his favorites (Flannery O'Conner, above all), dismissed lazy opinions, and encouraged us all to read with both objectivity and passion. His voice had a distinct timbre, a slightly raspy tenor that would fall an ominous octave or so when you were put on notice that your judgment was suspect, and would rise whenever he laughed, with the puckish sense of humor of a born mischief-maker. We were all more than a little terrified of disappointing him, whether by being lazy or obtuse, but his classes were clearly the highlight of everyone's week.

I got to know John much better the following year, when he became my thesis advisor, which led to frequent meetings in his office. Those hours were a delightful mix of department gossip, John gently ridding me of the remnants of my Midwestern ya-hooness, and his criticism of my thesis-in-progress. Whatever I've learned about writing and editing, I learned in those sessions. My topic was postwar fiction, and he informed me early on that he had little use for the writers I had chosen as subjects. "*No* one is going to be reading these people in twenty years!" he'd say impatiently, but humored me all the same. (He was, in fact, mostly correct about that.) His editing of my drafts was so insightful that he'd have me laughing when he pointed out egregious examples of my enthusiastic undergraduate pretensions.

The year after I graduated I returned to the Bay Area for a short vacation and had dinner with John. "Well," he asked me during the course of the meal, "what are you planning on doing now?" I'd been working as a paralegal for the past few months, a job I enjoyed, and replied, "I'll probably go to law school." The look John gave me could serve as a perfect dictionary illustration for "askance," and he said firmly, "No! No law school. You should be an editor. I'll write you a recommendation for the Radcliffe Publishing Course, and then you should look for a job in publishing." I was taken aback. At that point in time, the idea of becoming an editor was about as inconceivable as becoming an astronaut, but John proceeded to explain why it would be a good fit for me.

Forty years have passed since then; I've worked at five different publishing houses, edited hundreds of books, worked with dozens of remarkable authors, and had the kind of gratifying career that, all those year ago, I could scarcely have had the imagination to conceive of on my own. I'll never know what John saw in me to urge me down this path, but scarcely a week passes that I don't consider what my fate might have been had I not had the privilege and pleasure of his friendship.

John passed away in April 2019, after a long struggle with Parkinson's. He capped a remarkable career of over five decades with four stories in *The New Yorker*; his collected stories, *The Heart Is a Full-Wild Beast* (A Public Space); and this final novel, *The Beggar's Pawn*.